INFINITELY
Small Things

Julie A.M. Hall

Infinitely Small Things by Julie A.M. Hall

Published by Julie A.M. Hall

Cover Design and Interior Layout by Ashley Santoro.
Editing by Kayla Ramoutar.

ISBN: 978-1-7778218-0-7 (print)
ISBN: 978-1-7778218-1-4 (eBook)

Printed in Canada
First Edition

For all my friends who live amongst the stars.

I hope you found peace.

I hope to know you again someday.

Thank you for sharing a small infinity with me.

CHAPTER ONE

Caspar

There was a familiarity in dying, a brief moment that would sing in my mind with my last thought, always along the lines of, oh, I remember this before the universe would take back what was rightfully theirs.

It was the encore they had so desperately cheered for; it was the crescendo in my chest as the curtains closed on an empty crowd and there was absolute nothingness left in the theatre but crushing silence.

It was the first thing I heard as my eyes opened to the flashlight being waved in my face, and then a few moments or seconds or hours of nothing. It was the silence I craved. The curtains had closed, my fingers poised over the keys and my abdomen moving with the sharp breaths I was taking. I settled onto the wooden bench and let myself feel the end. I let my fingers graze the keys ever so lightly so as to play a whisper of the song, one that only I could hear. I wouldn't share it with anyone, the show was over, and I had nothing but emptiness and freedom. I was, for seconds, for what seemed like brief moments in time—completely and utterly weightless.

I knew it was over again, and the song was gone the next time my eyes opened.

The darkness was replaced with stark white, crisp smells of cleaning supplies that left a tang in your nostrils, and then the urge to spill my guts hit faster than my hands could reach for a bin. I barely had time to lean over the bedrail and send my dinner to the plain tiled floor.

Laughter. I heard tiny giggles and a snort as I wiped the vomit from my chin and peered at the woman across from me. My eyes had blinked once, twice, three times and still were not adjusted to the brightness in the room. I yearned for the silence to return as my ears felt as though they were bleeding from all the noise they were trying to decipher. My attention slipped back to the small woman who dressed in white, covered in a thick wool blanket of many colours.

She was wrinkled, the kind of wrinkled that makes you dread growing old. The kind that made people assume she made the best chocolate chip cookies and had over five grandchildren, all of whom she had pictures of in her ruby red purse which happened to sit on the small table next to her bed. Her glasses had to have been at least an inch thick and set in frames of bright pink plastic. The eyes behind them stared at me as she offered a silent apologetic nod in my direction and waved.

"Is something funny?" I managed to croak. My throat felt so dry that I swallowed, and it felt like sending tiny bits of sand down my esophagus.

Her brows knit together. "I was just thinking," a smile tugged at the corners of her mouth, "about the irony of you wanting to die, and me having no choice except to die."

I scowled at the no-doubt mad woman with the pink glasses, and turned onto my side, the crisp hospital linens scratching at the bracelet on my wrist. I yearned to hear the music again, to feel the weightlessness of death in my chest again, but it was replaced with steady beeps and an itch from my forearm where an IV line protruded. Pain started to register in the corners of my mind, and I groaned.

"Does it hurt?" A quiet question, from a tiny lady.

"What?" I managed, my voice sounding foreign as my ears still strained to adjust.

"Dying. Did it hurt?"

I propped myself up on my elbows and narrowed my eyes in her direction. She just stared at me, questions in those pink spectacles, and waited.

I don't know how long we just stared at each other, perplexed. Suddenly there were monitors beeping from behind the curtain to my left, and I realized there were four people in the room. I tuned out the sounds as nurses and doctors rushed in. There was still vomit on the floor next to the bed; I cringed and looked away, eyes darting until I looked to the small table next to the bed which held my belongings. I quickly picked up the cellphone and plugged-in headphones. It was not until the third song on shuffle that I noticed that wrinkled face was still staring at me, no doubt waiting for an answer to her question poised moments ago.

"Not nearly as much as being alive."

I don't know how loud I had said it, it felt like a scream erupting from my chest.

The woman in pink glasses smiled at me and returned to reading a book that was resting at the foot of her bed, adjusting those peculiar frames up the ridge of her crooked nose. I swore I caught her smiling at me over the next few hours, in between scrolling on social media and skipping songs on the playlist I was tuned into, hoping the guy in the room next to me was alright.

A while later, the doctors and nurses left the curtains closed to the section of the room where the monitors were frantic hours ago, replaced by silence. I took out one of my earbuds out of morbid curiosity. One of the nurses spotted the vomit on the ground and stopped at my bedside.

"Is there anything I can get for you?"

I shook my head.

"The Social Worker will be by in a few hours, and then you will be eligible for discharge. Just push the button if you need anything." She motioned to a small red button attached to the side of the bedrail.

I nodded, and she was out the door in a whirl of blue scrubs and shampoo. I think she was my nurse last week too. I remember the way she didn't meet my eyes and instead stared at the scars on my arms.

"What's your name, child?" the old woman asked over the spine of her book.

I didn't answer for a few breaths. Instead, I listened to the quiet, and could finally hear myself in my head, instead of the sheerness of the sounds coming from the other quadrant of the stale room. I could make out a quiet stream of violin coming from an antique looking wooden box next to the old woman. For a moment I stared at the wooden box, wondering if the sound would strike a match in my soul and light my lungs on fire. It was like holding my breath underwater, as the song spiked and then eased into the next tune, predominantly somber.

"Caspar," I breathed, out of relief for the music playing through my ears.

She hummed in response, and flipped through the pages of her book, a few strands of her grey hair falling loose from the braid she had tucked behind her head.

"Caspar, ah here you are. Of Persian decent,

loosely translated to keeper of treasures, blah blah blah, uptake in popularity during The Friendly Ghost era of course," a small giggle erupted from her mouth, "Oh! Caspar of Tarsus brought the infant Jesus a gift of gold while in the Manger, always wondered what they expected a newborn to make of that kind of a present. I mean you would think maybe a comfy crib, but no, let's just bring a big old hunk o'gold to the wee babe!" She proclaimed the last sentence and smiled at me over the book, which I now saw the spine read The Name-o-Saurus in bright bold text.

I stared at the woman in utter disbelief. It was definitely starting to seem like the strangest suicide hangover day. I had dubbed it The Day After the Music Hit Its Peak when I hit rock-bottom and wanted out, but not quite enough to stay in that blissful backstage scene post-encore performance. I always came back.

"What treasure are you keeping, boy?"

"Why do you call me those things, boy,

child?" I sneered in her direction.

"Would you prefer friendly ghost?" A sly smile.

One that, to my surprise, suddenly pulled at my own mouth. I tried to hide it, out of fear of the woman perceiving my smile as the opportunity to continue this interaction. I was saved by the nurse whose face I vaguely recognized as she whirled into the room; I half expected her to ask me if I was okay again before she went straight for the woman, whose mouth was open, no doubt another joke headed my direction.

"Mrs. Farid?" she asked the woman.

"Please dear, call me Ansa." A wink in my direction, and I truly thought myself mad. I must have still been overdosing, a blend of too many pills sloshing around my brain cells making me imagine strange people and even stranger conversations.

"Ansa," the tired nurse sighed, "the chemo clinic called, they are ready for us to bring you downstairs now."

The nurse did not wait for a reply and simply started readying a wheelchair and disconnecting nearby monitors. I wondered if that was the problem in this world; everything always moved so fast. There was no time, it seemed, for moments to truly be felt. The small woman looked afraid for half a second, and I swear I could feel the fear as it beckoned out for someone to recognize, to hold her hand and tell her that it would be okay. I could see it, just for a flicker of time. I don't know if this extremely peaked sense of mine, of noting the small changes in behaviour in those around me, was a blessing or a curse.

As soon as that fear melted away, she was back to making jokes with the young nurse, making conversation, genuinely interested in the forced one-word answers that were returned to her. It was like watching a volleyball game, in which one person fought so hard to play and to keep the game as it was supposed to be played, as the other sat on the ground on the other side of the net and built a sandcastle. Lost in her own thoughts, and completely unaware of the shouts coming from the other side of the net, desperate for someone to toss the ball back over, so she could keep smiling. But the favour was never returned, and I watched as the ball rolled under the bleachers, and the woman in the pink glasses, Ansa, transferred from the small bed into the wheelchair.

She was no more than 90 pounds, with small limbs and a short stature. But her face held so much more. I watched her pack up her belongings with the help of the nurse, and wanted to know the meaning behind her name.

I yearned for the chance to play a game of verbal volleyball with this tiny person, yet I had no idea why. I had not felt the desire to do much of any-thing for a long while. Especially not when I was within the hospital walls.

Ansa removed her pink spectacles and set

them down on the side table. It was strange that she was leaving them behind. The nurse did not notice as she looked at a message on her small pager and ushered the woman to settle into the wheelchair so they could be on their way, and so she could move on to the next task.

As Ansa settled in, she smiled at me once more. I noticed she was beautiful, not in the way you may look at models but in the way you look at people who have changed the world. The way that makes you think, that was a person you wanted to get the chance to know.

As the nurse wheeled her out of the room, moving past the foot of my hospital bed, she looked at me with a wild grin on her face.

"Boo!" She laughed, a short one on a short breath, and waved at me as the nurse took a call on her phone and quickly moved out of the room.

My eyelids felt heavy, and I surrendered to sleep.

CHAPTER TWO

Ansa

I wondered if I would see that boy again, with his sad eyes and scarred skin. I wondered if I would know what it truly felt like to die, before experiencing it for myself.

I had asked the nurse her name. "Jessica" was all that she said, and I could tell she did not particularly want to speak. So I stayed quiet and began to think about all the people I had met named Jessica. It was not a particularly big list; I could see images of school friends, and colleagues, and then nothingness. I could not recall what the name meant, or its origins.

It was a hobby I started when I first found out the cancer had spread. I knew I did not have much longer and I wanted to learn as much as I could. I wanted to fill my head with useless information, spout it off like a dictionary before taking my final breath, and be able to sleep soundly forever knowing that I had taken in as much life as my lungs could possibly allow.

It started with learning about different cultures, learning their histories, then learning about people throughout time. I loved learning the stories of others. I wanted to craft them into a blanket that would cover me and keep me safe from the darkness ahead. I wanted to talk with them, to find out what it had felt like to invent electricity, or what it felt like to walk on the moon. I wanted to learn about every possible feeling this human vessel could behold.

And then my daughter died.

You see, when you are wrapped up in the world of cancer and the inevitability of death you forget about the cruel quickened fates of things such as car accidents and tragedy. Death seems predictable because you know it will soon be knocking at the front door. So, when it blasts through the chimney like Kris Kringle on the 22nd of May, wearing black and holding a scythe—it shatters reality. It shattered everything I knew.

Elena was the epitome of her name. I remembered when her father and I held her and whispered her name into existence. It was as if the light of day shone from within that small baby's face, as she realized who she was to become. Elena, the illuminator. Elena, the very rays of sunshine that kept the world turning on its axis.

Without her, the sun had no warmth. Without her, there was just darkness.

I was about to ask the girl her mother's name, when she stopped abruptly at the door to the chemotherapy unit of St. Bartholomew's Hospital. Probably a good thing, as I realized the question may have been too intrusive.

"Can you walk a few steps?" Nurse Jessica

asked.

"That depends on the size of shoes." I smiled up at her face which did not reflect a mirrored image.

She did not hear the joke, or if she did it did not show on her face, and instead pushed the wheelchair access button next to the double doors and they whooshed open for her to push me through. She paused a couple steps into the room before continuing to the registration desk by herself, leaving me in one spot like a child waiting for their parents to come fetch them from daycare.

I waved as she disappeared through a separate exit door, and a different nurse came to bring me to my room. It was a small room, separated by curtains and not wall.

The smell hit me like a wall of bricks, and I scrunched up my nose. Stale vomit, mixed with chemicals and sterilization. I turned my attention to the male nurse who was now connecting the wires and leads to the monitors nearby.

"How are you today?" he smiled at me.

"As well as can be, thank you for asking my friend."

"My name is Henri," he waved a hand towards his ID tag pinned to his scrubs, "and I will be your nurse today during treatment. We have you down here for an hour today and then I have been informed a bed has become available on our Palliative floor."

He meant well, and I found myself smiling at the hopeful youth before me. I know he did not think about what it meant that someone earlier today was in that very same bed. I shuddered and pushed the thought away.

"Henri, spelt with an I—French?" I asked.

He grinned ear to ear, clearly proud of his heritage. "Mais oui, Madame."

He offered a squeeze to my hand before telling me to push my call bell if I needed anything and flicking the bag of fluids that would try to ease the spread of the illness in my body. He left the room with a small skip to his step, and I wondered how people could do this job. I think I would be a lot more like Jessica; I do not know how people face death so often and so willingly on a daily basis and still manage to walk with their shoulders straight and chin up.

That boy—I heard the doctors when he was brought into the Emergency room, where they had me waiting for more permanent hospital lodging—they said he had overdosed on pain killers and anti-depressants. They seemed to know him, I even heard one of them refer to him as a frequent flyer. I wondered what merits you had to have to be a part of that club and if you got discounted flights.

But he was nothing like I would have expected from a man who met death moments ago. He woke and then he seemed to instantly want to sleep again, seemed pained to have been woken from that sleep, and I wondered for the first time if maybe death was not so bad after all.

Since I had to bury my daughter last year, since the last time I heard her mutter something at me or tell me to hush, ever since the last time I saw Elena's bright eyes, I had worried more about dying. Before, it seemed natural. At my young age of just 86 I thought it would be fitting that I would be diagnosed with cancer, fight as hard as I could and then eventually just not be here any longer. But at least I knew Elena would speak my name, would tell my grandchildren about me, would cry over photos of me and her father at our wedding.

Now, it was as if I was dying twice over.

They say you die twice—the first when you take your last breath, and the second time, the last time that somebody earthside mentions your name.

What if there was nobody left earthside? Your name would become nothing.

That was where it had started with names. I began wanting to know more about the whispers your name breathed into your soul. I came across a journal, published sometime in the 1800s by philosophers that said a name bore your soul rather than the other way around. It shared that we were all connected through names, and that if our name did not match our soul, we would be pulled apart from the inside, muscle by muscle.

My stomach coiled at the grotesque thought, and I started to set up my room. I could walk, it was slow and looked as though my knees would give way at any moment, but I still wanted to do things myself as long as I could. I felt a wave of guilt for joking with that nurse Jessica and making her think I could not walk. I noted to apologize if our paths crossed again before mine careened off the side of a cliff.

I found myself entranced by the drip, drip, drip of the IV line combined with the soft piano music coming from the small radio I placed beside my bed.

I let the music carry me into sleep, willing the medication to stop fighting.

Truth was, I wanted to stop fighting. There was a war raging in my veins between the deadly spread of the cancer cells and the healing powers of modern medicine.

But then in the middle of the battlefield, I could see my daughter and my husband. I ran right between the armies waving a white flag and collapsed into the feeling of hugging my family.

When I woke the next time, I was not hooked up to any monitors, and I was in a room with floral wallpaper and a much more comfortable bed. I thought maybe this was it, maybe I had made the journey and the great beyond had strange interior design choices. Until I saw the IV pump in the corner and my belongings on a dresser across from me. What I did not expect was to see a ghost peering at me, leaning on the door frame to the small room, with questions in his eyes pleading for me to answer, clutching a pair of pink rimmed glasses in his hand.

"Boo!" he said, with a small grin.

CHAPTER THREE

Caspar

The Social Worker spent about ten minutes asking questions about my thoughts and gave me all the information about resources which she knew she had given me last time. Our small-town hospital only had the funding for one mental health professional it seemed, and I often found myself feeling bad for the woman.

She cared; it was obvious. I could only imagine what taking on the level of pain that would be brought about by these consults would wreak on her life outside of this building. I knew she wanted to spend more than ten minutes, wanted to talk for longer and heal those deep traumas she knew were brewing under my skin, but she probably already had five other younger kids she had to see before going home for the day, and maybe they were first timers. I could see the plea in her eyes as she handed me pamphlets with crisis phonelines on them and gave me her business card which included a cell number. She probably never truly left work, and I tried to promise myself next time to call her beforehand, at least give her a brief moment of feeling as though she could make a difference.

I smiled, and we shook hands, and she accidentally said, "hope to see you soon, Caspar."

She realized what she had implied, and threw an apologetic look my way, which I met with a smile and a nod as she turned on her heels and was off to try and play superhero for someone more likely to accept the gift of being saved.

The clock showed it was five in the evening. I had been here just one night. Just last night I had died and now I was changing out of the hospital gown and into my grey hooded sweatshirt and faded blue jeans. For someone who had celebrated going around the sun twenty-six times this weekend, the person in the hospital bathroom mirror appeared no stronger or wiser than a little boy. I tied my long black hair back into a soft bun, crested atop my head. My mother had loved my hair, she would comb it and sing songs to me as a boy. I never had the desire to cut it anywhere shorter than halfway down my back, always hearing those lullabies whenever scissors were near my head. Besides the long hair, there was nothing very distinguishable about the man in the mirror.

I pulled the hooded sweater over my right arm, and I found myself staring at the wide scar etched along my wrist and up my forearm. I stared at it and felt the waves of sadness crash against my skull.

It had been over two years now. The last time I was able to float over the keys and create those sounds, with all ten fingers taking on their own roles in filling the silence. It was an orchestra of sorts, comprised of nothing but the sounds of fingers on keys and nothing in between.

Lost in thought, I heard a sharp rap at the door; another patient waiting for the washroom.

I gave an apologetic nod and went to pull my sneakers on at the side of my bed when I saw the sun glint off the pink frames on the bedside table adjacent me.

Ansa, the name echoed in my skull.

Before I even knew what I was doing, I was in that doorway, staring at her tiny body nestled underneath the multicoloured blanket. I wondered if she had made that blanket herself. As if I had posed the question aloud, the woman peered out of the sheets, and our eyes met and held each other as if looking into a mirror. I wondered why I was feeling so inclined to get her to smile in that moment. I thought I saw a glimpse of the same darkness I'd seen in my own eyes before the end, and so I broke the silence with a single word.

"Boo," was all I could manage.

I felt as though I knew the woman, as if she was a story my mother had told me about.

I also felt as though I was mad.

I shook my head. "You forgot these," I said, waving the pink framed glasses, "I thought you may need them."

"Do you see people you've lost?" she asked, softly.

She seemed different, tired. As if the woman who was joking with me earlier was a mask and this was her true self. I remembered the first question she had posed, hours earlier. *Does it hurt?*

"It doesn't hurt."

"Interesting, will you always answer a previous question? Do I have to be one step ahead at all times with this generation?"

I shrugged. "I thought you deserved a better answer."

She motioned for me to come further into the room. "Come and sit, if you'd like. I could use the company."

I ignored the offer and remained in the doorway.

"Good luck with everything," I said, instead. I walked a few feet into the room, forcing my feet across the floor. I set down the glasses carefully on the small table next to her bed.

She reached out for my hand, but I pulled away and was out of the door before any more words could be exchanged. I navigated through the hospital the same way in which the administration desk had informed me to find Ansa, as I told them I was a grandson. I don't know why I had lied, why I had not just given them the glasses and her name and let them toss them in a lost and found bin.

I don't know why the pitter-patter of rain as I exited the main emergency doors reminded me of the way the old woman had laughed, and why I hoped to have the chance to find out what her name meant. I shook my head and pulled the hood over my hair before catching the first bus to pull up outside the doors.

Whitegate was a small town nestled on the eastern shore of Cork Harbour in County Cork, Ireland. It was home now, though not always. I had grown up in a small town in British Columbia, Canada. The water smelled the same here, which I think is why I had decided to stay last year, when what was supposed to be a soul-searching trip turned into finding a little apartment by the water and trying to find a new purpose.

I slid into one of the seats on the crammed bus and pulled my cellphone out of my pocket. The screen was empty, void of the missed calls that no doubt would have been there a few years ago. I could see her at the phone, hunched with worry trying to get a hold of me.

I breathed out a sigh, the smell of the sea

waking me up from a nap against the cold glass window just in time to get off down the street from the apartment.

The streets were mostly empty and so blissfully quiet. I walked between alleyways and found myself kicking rocks into the shoreline and letting my hair down from its bun. I took deep inhales and let the citrus and seawater scent carry me into a blanket of warmth despite the cold rain bouncing off my face.

I took the long way home, and when I saw a small girl holding hands with her mother, leaving the bank with pink glasses nestled against her face, I thought again of the peculiar twenty-four hours that had passed. It felt like a separate reality for some reason. I let the thoughts go before climbing the steep hill to get to the four-room apartment building I lived in. I checked the mail, more so out of feeling like it was the normal thing to do; nothing ever really came.

When I opened the front door, the first thing

I saw were the pill bottles. They were thrown about, even some pills left lying in different spots. A few of them on the counter, a few on the floor. I swept them up into their respective bottles, having the colours and sizes memorized after these years of rehabilitation and recovery.

The accident shattered my arm in three spots, and they had to put seven screws in to hold the bones in place while they mended. The pain was something of another world. I remember begging and pleading for them to increase my pain medications so often during those first few weeks after surgery. It was like there was a fire in my bones and the pills were the only thing that would calm the cruel lick of flames against the nerve endings that were screaming in agony.

I also remember the first time I used the pills for different reasons. It happened slowly at first, with a few nights of restless sleep, a few people that I saw who reminded me of my mother, a few nightmares.

My arm no longer ached, but the flames still licked at the pain receptors in my brain, and I knew I was out of options. It was the pills or lie awake at night while being filled with despair.

I told myself it was just until I could get stuff figured out, until I could properly mourn my mother and move on. I lied to myself. I lied to my doctors and told them my arm was still on fire and I couldn't get any sleep the pain was so bad, so they kept prescribing and I kept taking.

It was the two-year anniversary of the accident, the violent car crash that ended her life and left me with this damned scar across my wrist. The first anniversary of the end of everything was the first time I took them to silence the music. The piano in the room was covered by a black blanket, and dust gathered on top of the sheet making it appear a lighter shade of darkness. I had not so much as uncovered the blanket overtop the piano until that night. I can remember the exact shade of grey as though it was the colour of the sky all the time, as though it was all around me. I tried so desperately to play the song she had taught me, I tried so hard, but my fingers wouldn't move—I was beyond repair. I was nothing, and I wanted all the noise in my head to stop. I wanted to see her again.

The paramedics brought me back every time. Seven times over the last two years I had died. Seven times I had needed to be brought back into existence by the hands and help from strangers. I don't know why I always called the number before taking the last mouthful. I think that was her, willing me to fight this curse and continue to live.

I hoped she could understand how badly that ache in my chest overcame that will to live. She was everything to me, she had always been everything. And now there was nothing, I was nothing.

Do you see people you've lost?

The question barked in my brain, as I collapsed onto the bed that took up the majority of my small apartment.

Hands clasped over my stomach, I pondered.

When the audience seemed empty, the final crescendo of music carrying the curtains closed, was it her I saw chanting my name over and over again, willing me to keep playing, keep the show alive and breathing?

Was it my mother I saw in the eyes of the paramedics as they shook my shoulders and pounded their hands against my heart? Was it her who breathed life back into my lungs?

I saw her then, the woman who worked so hard to give me a good life, the woman who protected me from harm at all costs, and I let tears roll down my face and smiled at her beautiful memory in my mind.

My mother taught me about my Indigenous roots but shielded me from the dark parts. She would talk about her time in residential schools, and she would tell me about the days she saw the darkness, but most often she would tell me the story about how her and my father fled.

The story was all I clung to. She would tell me of the smell of the forest, of his hand in hers, of the sweet smell of the water that told them they were close to freedom. They made it back home and were hidden, eventually choosing to live off reserve in Victoria, British Columbia. They survived that journey, but then cancer came along and took my father from her before he could even hold their sweet baby boy and tell their story together.

And how unfair of Mother Earth then to come along and tear away such a warrior of a woman by having her cross paths with a drunk driver and be ripped away from her child.

I had work in the morning and wanted to get the stench of the hospital out of my hair before climbing under the covers and trying to close my mind to the world.

But even as the steam from the shower trickled over my hand, I felt the question echoing through my mind, and I knew I had to go back to answer it in person. Because the truth was… I think I had seen her. I could see her in the middle of that empty theatre, hands clasped over her heart, and I wanted to tell someone else that I had seen her. I needed to tell that woman that there was hope, I owed it to myself to give her that. I hoped that someone would show me the same kindness on my deathbed.

I willed myself into bed, but before I closed my eyes, I ran a google search for the name Ansa.

It was Urdu, a Muslim name—for purest love.

I set my alarm an hour earlier than need be.

CHAPTER FOUR

Caspar

There was a moment I stared at the alarm clock blinking 6:00, where I thought maybe the power had gone out. I rubbed at my eyes and yawned, before remembering the reason I had set the alarm earlier than normal for my shift at the oil refinery. I worked in their marketing department, a mundane 9-5 that was never really anything more than making rent in time.

If you would have asked me how early I had gotten up to be in class, to be at rehearsals, or grad school auditions, you would not have believed the glee in my eyes as I told you of hours you probably had no idea even existed.

Long gone were the days of inspiration, and

I wondered why I had bothered this morning. Why was I bothering with any of this? These past two years I had been hospitalized, tossed in and out of emergency rooms like hotel rooms, like they were giving away brand new cars with every stomach pumping. Never before had I gone back to visit with an old neighbor. There was a brief moment where I considered Ansa would be surrounded by loved ones at her bedside, who would ask who I was and why I was staring at their dying grandmother and wanting to talk with her. Just as quickly, I had remembered the look in her eyes that I had recognized. She had asked me if you see those who you've lost, the people who you had loved most and left you Earth Side.

And I recognized that small flickering rage in her eyes, the one that signalled a recent tragedy that evoked pain worse than the dark cloaked figure hiding in the IV pumps.

I recognized that same flicker from my own eyes on each of the seven occasions I had tried to kill myself. I think that was one thing I always struggled with, putting a label on it. Sometimes I would tell myself it was an accident, but I knew the truth deep down inside. Running the risk, it was a little too much for my body to handle, was just the same as putting a bullet in my foot and running a marathon.

I was trying to die, really and truly. But those damn pink glasses, they had more to share. With that thought, I hauled my jacket on and started the lengthy detour to St. Bartholomew's Palliative Care Center.

When I first told the lie, it had felt wrong.

"Who are you here to see, sir?" The same auburn-haired receptionist asked me, glancing above the screen of her computer.

"Ansa Farid, in 216." This time, it felt right.

She offered to show me the way, remembering me from yesterday afternoon—she told me that my grandmother had been moved to a room a few spaces down the hallway. I told her I would find the way and jotted down the number 222 on the back of my hand.

Although I knew the emergency room that was connected on the other side of the brick wall, the hospital seemed like a different universe. The first thing I noticed was the soft piano music, which played from the speakers, instead of the constant beeping that filled the space I had been officially dubbed a frequent flyer. The second thing I noticed was the colours; where the hospital was a crisp white, like the first snowfall of the year, this was utterly autumn. The hallways all changed colours, none painted perfectly, none really having matching carpeting and drapery, but it felt like it was alive. Ironic, as I knew what I had read on the sign outside the main doors.

The third thing I noticed ran into me.

I mean, she was busy juggling about a dozen small easels and jugs of paint. I did not help the situation much as I was too busy thinking about how an interior designer would react to the different colours everywhere and the overcrowded bulletin boards falling on the floor. When we collided, all the canvases and paint fell from her hands.

"Oh!"

I caught her elbow and steadied her, before instantly bending down to scoop up the dropped materials. There were pieces of canvas glued to the easels. They were half completed, a variety of images. There was so much colour.

"I am so sorry!" She seemed to yell every word.

"No apologies needed," I handed her the stack of easels, "I was in my own little world, probably swerved into your lane"

She giggled, and I mean a giggle. The kind you'd expect from a toddler who has learned their very first curse word. I smiled at her and placed the final easel I had collected on top of the pile she held.

"Trust me, if anyone is in their own little

world around here, it's this lady."

She flung two pointed thumbs in her own direction, balancing the easels against her body and her elbows tucking them in. I found my mouth curving upwards. I took a moment to take in what was standing in front of me. She appeared to be in her twenties, but her face held the lines of worry worth many more. It was like the smile pressed outward made her age in the most beautiful way. She had a literal rainbow sprouting from her head. A twisted creation of pipe cleaners nestled between two lazily placed buns atop her head. Then a pink polka dot tee peeked out from behind the paint splattered apron she donned. She was not wrong; she clearly belonged to nobody but her own little world.

"I'm Tessa, have I met you yet?" She left no time for a reply. "No, I haven't met you yet! Who are you?"

An overhearing nurse wearing scrubs with cats on them snickered in our direction and offered me a warning glance. "Boy, you best run before this one gets you to make a mural or talk about your feelings."

It felt like I was on a soap opera, and I decided to listen to the advice given, offering a nod in their direction and turning on my heels. I heard the women laughing and chatting behind me as I resumed scanning room numbers, looking for the digits that matched the back of my hand. I passed the room she was in a few nights ago, and it was empty. I wondered if someone had come and gone already. I shuddered.

I came to the room and peered around the corner, and imagined I looked like a criminal for certain.

She seemed like she was actively shrinking, and as soon as I saw her eyes were closed, I started to turn around and come back the way I came. I knew I would probably cross paths with the rainbow woman again, but I decided it would be less awkward than waking a woman on her deathbed, when I had spoken all of two words to her.

"The ghost returns." A small cackle of laughter echoed from just behind me, in the room.

"Why did you ask me those things?" I blurted out. It was like the words had been loaded in my throat from the time I left the loft.

She propped herself up in bed using the remote control attached to the bedrail.

"I wanted to know," she said, "I wanted to know if I can expect to see my family or to see nothing."

"And you thought a suicidal man would know best?"

"Would you prefer if I told you it was an attempt to flirt?" The woman was old enough to be my grandmother, but she said this jokingly with a wink in my direction.

"No. Definitely not." We laughed together for a moment.

"How do you do it without any fear?"

I walked into the room a few paces and shrugged.

"I guess when you don't feel anything at all—fear is included in that."

She looked me up and down. "You know, you look like my daughter."

"Poor thing," I offered.

This time she was laughing so hard that she coughed, and I felt guilty for making the joke. She was so small in that bed and looked as though she could breathe her last breath at any moment.

"The name Aiyana means eternal flower."

She smiled at me, a silent question looming in her eyes.

"My mother," I offered the answer to her long-ago asked question, "I see her every time. She doesn't look the same though, she is my mother, but she is also much more. She is glowing, and she simply looks…"

I struggled to find the word, my palms turning upwards to the woman in the pink glasses.

"Eternal," she offered, and I nodded.

She had seemed eternal each of the times I saw her. She welcomed me with open arms, she held me in the darkness after the curtains closed on my show.

My heart felt like it would cave in, and I think the woman sensed this as she gestured to the chair next to her bed.

I called my boss and told him I had the flu, marking the third lie I had told that day.

CHAPTER FIVE

Tessa

I asked Lorraine, my lovely Charge Nurse and keeper of all the gossip on the unit, who that new man was, and who he was seeing.

"He is visiting with 222, I saw him here last night too, Grandson probably."

"I have to find time today to go meet her, she came in from emerge last night, right?"

A nod, and a sip of coffee and I was on my way to the morning painting class I instructed. Lorraine shook her head as I scrambled down the hallway, sneakers squeaking on the tiled floors every step of the way. I fixed my hair before opening the doors.

There were about ten patients who smiled at me, and I returned their smiles as I started handing out hellos along with brushes.

"Good morning, Tessa, dear."

"Good morning, Mrs. Dove, how are we feeling today?"

"Blessed."

I smiled and continued handing out easels and getting my group all set up.

"I think I want to start a new one today." Herb frowned at the half-finished sunset image he had been working on this week. "It just does not feel right anymore."

I nodded and handed over a blank canvas, and purposefully set my own half-finished portrait of a bridge over a stream of colours, right next to him. Just in case he needed to talk.

"Can I get anyone a glass of juice, cup of tea or anything before we start?"

We sat there for the first twenty minutes in silence, everyone focused on their artwork. Gradually, chatter started to fill the silence. Herb told me about his son finally coming to visit him over the weekend, about how happy he was to have had the chance to say goodbye. He wanted to paint a sunrise instead of a sunset, and I thought that was so utterly beautiful that I had to bite back the urge to burst into tears and scare the wits out of the group of senior citizens painting around me. He reached for my hand and thanked me. I squeezed the leathery skin and could tell he meant it. I was not quite sure what I had been thanked for, sometimes I had to take time to think about things said to me here. I was okay with that though; I had learned to live in the moment and take time to enjoy those infinitely small moments in time where life stilled for people to talk.

An hour came and went, and nurses flooded the room to return their patients to the respective rooms. I reminded everyone of the balloon badminton game we had on the schedule this afternoon, and the reading circle which would follow.

I wheeled Herb back to his room myself, an-other usual. He was one of Lorraine's patients, and she knew I always returned him—usually late, but we always came back.

"You want to get a coffee?" But I was already heading to the cafeteria, and Herb knew.

"I think I may try a green tea today; Marge never shuts up about its healing properties. Maybe I will walk back to my room!"

I snorted a laugh; Marge was the small lady who always talked to other patients on the floor about her homeopathic cancer treatments. She meant well, but she sounded off her rocker crazy most days. Some people would get actually angry with her no-tions, but most of us knew that the only reason she shared her opinions and thoughts was out of hope. All she wanted was to live and feel good, not the kind of feeling you get after a hefty dose of chemo-therapy. We understood her, but that did not mean we did not poke fun.

"Be nice." I tapped him on the shoulder and Herb laughed.

He put his hands up in defense, and we chatted about his visit with his son the rest of the morning. We sat across from one another in the cafeteria of the main hospital and watched as nurses and doctors flooded the room as shift change hour neared. It was curious to see some people fill their mugs with coffee, and others start to unpack lunches. It was as though we were all in our own time zones, despite being in the same room. We knew Lorraine would be upset at his tardiness for medication pass, but we still opted to take a stroll through the gardens on the way back to our little space on the opposite end of the hospital. It was mid-April and the air smelled of the sea, and flowers were just starting to sprout from the ground. It was a warm day, and we picked a bench next to a cement birdbath.

"Does the red hair make you the original

Irish? I half expected to be in a sea of red-heads when I came here with my wife."

I rolled my eyes. "My accent should be a clear give away that I am as originally Irish as it gets there, Herbert."

He loved to make jokes, and I think that was why he was one of my favourites. We were never supposed to have favourites; all my schooling told me to avoid getting too close to our patients and always maintaining a professional boundary to reduce burnout. But they never told us in school how hard that would be, how hard it was to ignore the stories that we related to.

How could you listen to someone on their deathbed, hold their hand as they crossed into the great beyond, and then go home to your family and not see their faces as you fell asleep?

So, I chose very early on in my career, to go all in.

I connected, I listened, and I took walks in

the gardens.

I cried and mourned them all. It was not easy, and where wedding season is usually a few months of the year, funeral season was not limited to any particular months.

I lived and breathed with them, and I helped them to live their last days with purpose, whatever it may look like for them. My title on my name badge was a recreation therapist, but I thought of myself more as a counsellor than anything else. I was here in whatever capacity they needed, and half the time they gave me more purpose than anything else.

"He has children, Tessa."

I furrowed my brows. "Your son?"

A small nod. "Two girls, and they have hair just like yours. A fire atop their heads, and a fire in their hearts. I get to meet them next weekend."

"I am so happy for you, Herb."

He reached up and placed his hand on top of mine which was pushing his wheelchair.

"I know."

Lorraine eyed us up as we both whistled away any guilt and strode by the nursing station with our backs straight and chins up.

She couldn't help the upward twitch of her mouth at the two troublemakers who passed her by. I helped Herb into bed and told him I would see him at balloon badminton this afternoon. He smiled and I noticed how it crinkled the corners of his eyes in a way it did not when I last saw him. His son had made that happen, I realized. It is miraculous how much of our lives is actually determined by the people around us, and by the love we choose to give.

After helping Herb to bed, I took a moment to myself in the washroom. I splashed some water onto my face and untied the two buns and adjoining pipe cleaner rainbow that I often did for our arts classes. It was starting to give me a headache as lunch neared, and I opted to let the red curls free for the afternoon.

I went to sit at a computer behind the nursing station and charted attendance at this morning's painting class before checking for new referrals. I worked on a referral basis with people in the main areas of the hospital, but most of my days were spent in our little home here on the palliative unit. I would automatically be referred to any new admissions to this floor, and I remembered about the man I crashed into in the hallway this morning. He had an unusually tanned complexion for someone in County Cork, or anywhere in Ireland for that matter. But he also had the most unusual expression for someone visiting a dying relative. He seemed curious and excited; it was like he was going to see a new movie he had heard about for so long. Most people walked these hallways with doom and gloom in their eyes, yet his were full of hope.

The referral was sitting unread in my emails, I printed off some documentation pieces and started my way towards room 222, unsure if I was going to meet a grandmother and her beloved grandson or if there was more to the story.

The room held a bit of history for me, as I was once the one in the bed. Childhood cancer had rocked my family when I was twelve and nothing was ever the same. Some things were better off, I felt this was what had led me to pursue my career dreams and to become a more empathic person over-all. I think only the people who have shook hands with death, understood what life really felt like. Funny how we have to be so close to losing something to recognize its worth. Some things were not so much appreciated, like the regular tests I get that invoke anxiety and PTSD. Part of me sometimes thought that I should have chosen a career path far away from the smells of healthcare settings, far away from the memories that would always come boiling back up in the back of my mind. But I took that thought and lit it on fire. I wanted to give back. The universe had given me a second chance, and it was something I would always be grateful for. Not many people got that second chance, so I felt as though I owed the universe and all those people who did not get it, everything. I had more left to do for the world, and what better way than helping those I could truly empathize with.

That's the thing. I don't think you really understand what death is until he is standing in the room with you. And sure, you may remember the first time your parents held your hands and dressed you in black and brought you along to Uncle Al's funeral, sorry Al, but that was different from experiencing the crushing presence of Death while someone was still breathing.

It was strange some days, walking into rooms and knowing that he was in the corner.

Telling people you would see them after lunch, and then finding out that they checked out when you were eating leftovers in the break room. Some days were harder than others; people like Herb usually caused the worse days. Not by any fault of their own—it was just that he had been here for a while, we had gotten to know him, we knew how much cream he took in his coffee, knew that he liked to get up around 9:45am, any earlier and good luck to the nurse trying to pry him out of bed. We knew his story. He was family, and he would die any minute.

It was living with that kind of sinking feeling in your chest that made you value every waking minute spent with them. That was why we walked through the gardens, and not the air-conditioned hallway.

When I was a patient, I remember the conversations I had with Death. I remembered the times he came close. I had aged a hundred years in the course of eight months. The promise of death is enough to rip away any remnants of childhood. Maybe that was why I had decided to always keep a piece of the girl who was in the bed in 222 with me, that was the pipe cleaner rainbow in my hair, she had done that this morning just to put a smile on the face of her patients. I think they half expected that sort of nonsense by now, certainly those like Herb who had been here a while now, but I caught him snickering at it when we were painting and that was a win for me.

It was something so small, but so filled with purpose that it become infinite. How does one quantify happiness? Infinitely small things, that's all we were. And if I could make those infinitely small things feel anything other than the lurking presence of Death in the corner of their rooms, well, that was all that mattered to this red-haired leprechaun.

CHAPTER SIX

Ansa

I was surprised to see him again. I really and truly thought he had written me off as some crazy old lady who asked him strange questions in the hospital.

But he was in the hallway, telling his boss he would not be in to work today. I wondered if I should make a joke about it, but when he sat down beside my bed all I could see in him was my daughter and I felt tears well up in my eyes.

"Your mother, how old were you when…?"

"Two years ago, there was a car accident." And the breath was taken from my chest.

"What date?"

He looked puzzled at the question. "May

22nd."

"It appears," I couldn't help but to sigh, "the universe has brought us together, my ghostly friend."

Again, he looked at me as if I was mad, and I laughed at the memory of Elena giving me the exact same look about thirty times a day in her teenage years.

"My daughter Elena, she would have liked you. Strangely enough, May 22nd two years ago she was taken from me just as your mother was from you. A head on collision with a long-haul truck driver who had suffered a heart attack while on his way home to his family for the weekend. I was so upset with that poor man, for so long. I blamed him. As if the poor man would have willed his heart to stop working for a beat in time."

Caspar leaned forward. "My mother's killer chose to pick up the bottle before his car keys. He didn't even have the chance to rot, he met the same fate as her."

"Don't speak ill of the dead, my boy," I warned.

"Why not?"

"You never know if your name will make you an easy target amongst the ghouls that roam the earth, what with the friendly attribute in all."

We laughed, and it was strange. It was like we had known each other forever, and I sensed that Caspar felt the same way.

"So, what," he gestured at the IV poles and surroundings, "brought you in?"

"Pancreatic cancer I am afraid, I've but a few weeks they say."

He wilted like a flower. "I am so sorry."

"People say that like they willed it upon me. I'm not sorry for dying. I'm sorry I waited so long to realize how important it is to truly be alive. That's why you perplex me, Caspar. Why would a man so fully able to continue living, simply want to die?"

"I already told you," he said, defensively.

"No, you gave an answer about not fearing death, or pain. You didn't say why you were so afraid of continuing to live."

"The reasons are too long to number a list." He laughed, but there was no joy.

"I have nothing but time, Caspar," I said, shrugging.

"Do you have any family?"

"My daughter was all I had left. My husband died ten years ago; lucky bastard just didn't wake up one morning. He didn't have nearly as much time to contemplate what lay ahead before he just ceased to be. Elena was devastated, a true daddy's girl from the first moment I handed her to him. She was so focused on schooling, she wanted to be a doctor you know. She was going to cure everything. Some months it was cancer, some it was ALS. She wanted to cure every possible tragedy."

I felt myself rambling and was surprised when I saw Caspar's eyes with that flicker again.

"What are you thinking about Caspar?"

"You said she would have liked me, why?"

"You are looking for the cures too. You just don't know it yet."

"You talk to me like you've known me for years." He didn't say it with a mocking tone, but a curious one.

"It feels like I have."

He nodded in agreement, and there was a small rap at the door that made both of our head's turn.

She was a firecracker of a woman. Red curls cascaded past her shoulders, and the smile on her face as she introduced herself as Tessa, seemed to reach her eyes in such an effortless action. I found myself pondering upon the etymology of the woman's name and wanted to ask her if it was a diminutive form of Theresa or perhaps even Esther. It could have come from two sources then, either the Greek *theros*, meaning "Summer", or *therizo*, meaning

"Harvester".

Caspar introduced himself as my grandson and I nearly spat the sip of water I had just taken, before nodding and extending my hand to the woman who looked like a mermaid. She apologized to him for earlier, and I made note of asking him all about that encounter, as well as why he referred to himself as my grandson.

"Mrs. Farid, it is a pleasure to meet you."

"The pleasure is all mine dear, please call me Ansa." We shook hands; hers was warm like she had just been outside tanning. The pale complexion and freckles adorning her nose and cheeks said other-wise.

"I am the recreation therapist here, which means I get to have all the fun. We have a calendar of events, and everyone is welcome to attend!"

She made every word sound like bread and honey; she spoke the way a mother would speak of her children. She was proud of what she did with her days.

I noticed the way she looked at the young man who I was starting to think of as a friend. I made a mental note to try and see if there was anything there before I surrendered to my demise, because that was the same way my husband had looked at me when we met. That was pure interest, and the kind of natural love that may just save this young man from meeting the end sooner than necessary.

She could be his semicolon, where he could have ended the sentence but decided to continue and persevere.

"What kind of things do you like to do to stay busy?"

"What is the next event on that calendar of yours, my dear?" I asked.

She handed me a large piece of paper, visibly excited at the question. Caspar stared at her too, and I noticed what a fool he really was. He so clearly wanted to live; he just did not have the guts to admit it.

I rolled my sleeves up and pointed at today's date. "Do we have to bring our own badminton racquets?"

Caspar raised his hands. "Oh, that's okay, just one racquet needed, I will stay here."

"Nonsense!" she trilled. "All family is welcome to join in as well!"

"Hear that grandson? We can play on a team!" I clapped my hands together, mocking him now as I saw fear flash in his eyes at how his day was unfolding.

I thought he may have pretended to take a call, but this man clearly had minimal social skills. Instead, he anxiously adjusted the hem of his hooded shirt and stuffed his hands into his pockets of his jeans.

Tessa smiled at me. "I am so happy to welcome you to our floor, please don't hesitate to reach out if you need anything, I am always around! There is a list of different activity kits I can put together for you to do independently as well, or if you want any church services at bedside, take a look through the lists and I can get you setup after the big balloon badminton match this afternoon. We play for cookies today!"

"Damn it, so there's no cash bets?" I laughed.

Tessa's whole face lit up. "You and I are going to become fast friends, Ansa!"

I agreed wholeheartedly, especially when she left, and Caspar was quiet for a few moments.

"When were you going to tell me you were my grandson? Is there a camera recording somewhere for some prank show?"

He smiled with a tinge of embarrassment I did not miss. "It's what I told them to get your room number."

"Well, I say," I said dramatically, putting a hand to my heart. "You went to such great lengths for a lady of my condition?"

"I just felt like we had more to say."

"And we do Caspar, we have a lot to say. Starting with the story of how you ran into the love of your life this morning?"

He stiffened in the chair, and I laughed heartily.

He shook his head, dismissing the comment for a joke. He would see, I was never wrong about that kind of stuff. Especially when two people were so obviously the same. Time was not on my side though, and I wanted to make this my last hoorah. I couldn't save Elena, but this boy was so clearly ready and willing to be saved.

I would do everything in my power to show him how much the world had to give to him, and the importance of learning to love. It was too late for me; I had realized that when I saw him in the emergency room. It seemed like so many days since the encounter but was only just shy of 24 hours ago.

I had lived my life as a quiet, small person.

I had refused to jump into the spotlight.

I was this boy, this ghost of a man who was clearly feeling so very small.

I had refused to love out of fear, I had discouraged going for your dreams, I had told my daughter it was impossible to take on such challenges of curing disease as one person, I had told our family I would not bother looking to love another man after my soulmate passed. Who knows what could have been different?

The world had been a massive place, a land in which were all tiny incognisant things. But I was wrong, and I knew that the moment I saw Caspar reduced to a shell of nothingness, so clearly yearning to live but needing a tether to the world. The truth hit me in that moment, which felt days ago already but maybe that was the impending clock of doom that sat in the back of my mind. From the moment I met this Caspar, I knew that the world is the tiny thing, and we are the big things. Without us, without love, it is nothing. We are the world.

I should have loved more.

That was the thought in my mind the whole night as I watched the boy and asked him questions simply to get him to speak, to connect.

And now, now I had made a friend.

And I believed now, that in the few days we would have—love would save us all.

CHAPTER SEVEN

Caspar

I was holding a plastic tennis racquet and swatting a balloon between seniors.

Did I mention I work a mundane job at the oil refinery here? I didn't usually spend my days like this. I spent my days here in County Cork mostly between my depressing loft and the equally depressing cubicle with no windows at my workplace.

So when the old lady across from me, who was clearly taking the game very intensely, gave me the middle finger for a bad swat of the balloon that resulted in it hitting the floor—I couldn't stop from laughing out loud. Had I lost my marbles, or was I in a movie?

The rest of the group broke into a fit of laughter as well, Tessa included. She was never not laughing or smiling though, I quickly noticed.

"Sorry!" I yelled across the makeshift circle.

"Oh, ignore crotchety old Marge, she doesn't know how to play nicely with new friends," the older gentleman next to her said, scowling.

Tessa swatted the balloon right at his face then, and his hands quickly shot up defensively.

"Play nicely, Herb," she snapped at the man before sticking her tongue out at him like she was five-years-old.

When we were finished our game of balloon badminton, the nurses were declared the winners, and I found myself starting to think of excuses for work tomorrow.

"Thank you all for coming out tonight, and a hearty congratulations to our caretakers, the Nurses, on their win tonight!" Tessa bowed at the nurses who were grouped around a table of snacks in the back of the small lounge. It was no bigger than my loft, and the art of getting all those wheelchairs into the tiny room was worthy of an award of its own.

"We have reading circle to follow, if some of you would like to stay, we are reading some community submitted stories tonight."

I looked at my watch and Ansa noticed, asking me to bring her back to her room before I left. It was strange, it was like at some point today a wall had broken down. We talked openly now, without fear of the other seeming crazy. I still had no inkling as to why exactly, but my heart told me I would eventually learn why I felt compelled to stay in this place.

I hadn't heard the music all day. I hadn't thought about the end, I hadn't taken any medications since this morning when I left the loft, I had not even thought about the ache in my arm. The soft jazz music that echoed through the hallways did not even make me feel on edge, and I felt goosebumps rise on my arms as I thought about why that may be.

We were almost at the doors, when a tap at my shoulder made me spin the wheelchair around much less gracefully than the nurses had when bringing people into the lounge.

"Leaving so early?" Tessa asked, a small pout on her face.

Ansa held her hand out to the girl. "We will be back tomorrow; what did you say is on the schedule again?"

Tessa grinned from ear to ear. "We have pet therapy in the morning, jazz-ercise in the afternoon, and an evening ice-cream social!" She waved her hands at her sides when she mentioned the Jazz themed exercise group, and I thought it was the silliest thing I had ever seen a grown woman do in public.

"Better than any five-star hotel I have ever stayed at!" Ansa laughed.

We joined her with a chuckle and exchanged goodnights before heading out of the lounge and into the hallway. We stopped to investigate some of the photos that littered the walls, glossing over the in-memoriam section, and were almost back to 222 when Ansa asked me to bring her outside for a few minutes first.

"I just want to have a cigarette."

"You—you what?" I sputtered.

"Want a cigarette, yes, and can I bum a lighter too please?"

I must have looked like my jaw was on the floor, because she added, "I am dying, you know."

"Trying to speed up the process?" I choked out in response.

"You can never speed it up or slow it down, Caspar, it only is what it is."

I put my hands up and figured it was just another stop on this whirlwind of a day. Ansa had noted an exit door on our way over to the lounge earlier in the afternoon.

The night air was crisp, the sunset must have

just dipped below the horizon. It was that time of day where the sky was unsure if it should turn out the lights. I loved the stories my mother would tell me about the sky, about our world. I was not raised entrenched in the Indigenous community back home, but my mother would tell me all the stories she was told by her mother and so on and so forth. She told me one day I would share them with my children, that it was how the world continued to turn; it was us that made it happen. Everything that happened in the universe, happened because and for us. We were the heartbeat of the earth. Inseparable.

That was what the sky reminded me of, the Seven Sisters.

I told Ansa the tale of the stars then, ignoring her request for a lighter for just a while longer in hopes I would not have to help an 86-year-old woman meet her expiration earlier than intended.

I pointed up. "Right below the grandmother spider is the Pleiades, the Seven Sisters. The Pleiades star group rises above the horizon soon after sunset and keeps a low trajectory above the horizon."

She nodded, sincere interest in her eyes under those pink frames.

I continued, "and that's called Pakone Kisik—you see?" I pointed to the spot where the edge of the sun crested over those Irish cliffs. "The hole in the sky, and the hole in the sky is where we come from."

I told her the rest of the stories I had been told by my mother. I told her all about the Star Woman who saw Earth from another dimension, fell through that hole in the sky because she fell in love, and became the first human on this planet.

"We come from the stars," I finished.

She looked at me, bewildered. "I am Hindu, and we say the stars of the Big Dipper were the seven sages called Rishis. These seven sages are always told to be the ones who make the sun rise and shine in the morning and fall and sleep at night. They were also happily married to seven sisters named Krttika.

It did not have as much of a happy ending, but…"

Now it was my turn to furrow my brows and contemplate. How could we be so many years apart, so many worlds apart, have just met under extremely different circumstances, and yet be told the same stories all our lives?

"Lighter?" She held her hand out.

I didn't even register what she had asked me for, perplexed about the stories we had shared with one another. I didn't have a lighter anyhow. I shook my head and was about to respond when Ansa snickered and mumbled something under her breath. I watched as Ansa, a small elderly woman with limited time, drew a cigarette out of her hospital sock, followed by a neon yellow lighter, and lit it.

She coughed so violently that I almost ran inside to get a nurse. She put a hand on my knee though and started laughing uncontrollably.

"I always thought I would detest them." She offered the cigarette to me.

I looked at her, bewildered, then put my hands up in refusal. I smoked a few years when I was a teenager, but only to try and fit in at school. I never really liked the taste or smell of them. Plus, my mother was excellent at pointing out the horrible death that would come to me if I continued smoking.

She shrugged and tossed the cigarette on the ground, rolling over it with her wheelchair a few times.

"I think that Tessa lady, she clearly came from a star."

I saw her cast a sideways glance at me and offered a small smile. I think she just may have been right.

I walked home that night, watching the night sky collapse onto us like waves crashing ashore. I watched the stars and recited the stories my mother had told me. She always tapped my chest when she said that we were a part of all stories.

When I got home, I was so tired I nearly forgot to take my medications before jumping into bed.

I saw the pill bottles that littered the floor near the covered piano and didn't feel the urge to take more than needed for the first time in a while. I saw them and I thought about the woman who had given me the middle finger, of the man who called her crotchety, or the pink glasses and—a new friend, I realized.

So, I took what was needed to numb the pain in my arm, and for the first time in a month I did the physiotherapy exercises that were recommended after my surgery. They said it would never be back to normal, but maybe there was a new normal for me.

Maybe this was just the middle of my story, a turning point so to speak. I don't know if it was my bipolar tendencies or the fact that the nurses schooled us in balloon badminton and I wanted revenge, but I felt connected to something. Not just to something, but to myself. I tapped myself in the middle of my chest, where my mother would have told me I was connected to everyone around me.

I let myself feel and cried myself to sleep that night.

CHAPTER EIGHT

Caspar

The next morning, my boss called to check in on me. I did my best impression of someone who had been up all-night vomiting, and to my relief, he told me to take a week so it didn't spread to anyone in the office. I thanked him and meant it. I felt like a different person that morning, and I quickly realized it was purpose that I was feeling. I had told Ansa I would be there in the morning in time for pet therapy and the rest of our planned-out day.

I also found myself wanting to take more pills than needed for the ache in my arm that morning. I stared at the pills on the countertop in my tiny kitchen and wondered what the point was. Why was

I forging a friendship with someone who would certainly cause me to feel more sadness in the very near future.

It took one look at the draped piano to feel the darkness creep into the corners of my mind. I felt my thoughts racing through memories of what it felt like to play the songs my mother had taught me. I felt the applause of an audience, the ricochet of my mother's whistling from the crowd. I missed brushing my hands over the keys and feeling complete. I crumpled the physiotherapy exercise instructions that were left on the countertop from last night as well.

I could feel myself wanting to lock the door and drown in the darkness. Maybe this would be the last time I would have to deal with the guilt of it, maybe this time I would be strong enough to make it permanent.

A bird chirped outside the kitchen window; it stared at me for a moment through the glass and I wondered if there would be pet therapy birds.

I didn't give the darkness another chance, tossing a jacket over the plain black tee and jeans I had thrown on. My hair was down today, its full length tickling my back slightly as I pulled my bike out from beside the apartment building entrance. I loved to feel the wind sweep my hair back as the air entered and left my lungs.

Free as the birds that fly, with their weightless souls.

It was a short ride, only five minutes or so until I was at that familiar sign surrounded by gardens.

Ansa sipped tea in her room, I spotted her through the window just as she spotted me.

A wicked grin spread across her face, and she threw up a middle finger in my direction.

I almost returned the gesture, before I noticed there were plenty of other people coming in and out of the doors and walking the grounds. She noticed my discomfort and I shook my head as the woman slapped her knee and laughed. I walked the entire rest of the way to her room with my head down, and the hood of my jacket up.

This time, nobody asked me who I was here to see, and the woman I had come to know as the leader of the nurse's troop, Lorraine, smiled and offered a wave. I waved and continued down the hallways until I reached the room with 222 scrawled on the door.

She looked sicker today; it shocked me how sunken in her eyes appeared underneath those pink glasses. She had the same goofy grin plastered to her face though, as she motioned for me to come closer. I smiled and leaned in the doorway.

"Do you have any manners?" Safely alone, I returned the middle finger gesture.

She laughed lightly. "Clearly neither of us do. How is the friendly ghost today?"

I contemplated telling the truth for a moment, telling her about the lengthy glances I took at the mirror or the pill bottles, telling her about how I had cried myself to sleep and then contemplated a more permanent sleep. I was so nonchalant about suicide though, and it made me just so damn embarrassed to tell a woman who was literally dying that I was sad.

But I was, and I think she knew by my hesitation.

"You missed the dogs," she tsked.

"Were there any birds?" I asked.

"Do you think such a thing exists? Therapy birds? Not particularly snuggly."

I shrugged. "I saw a bird this morning."

She was about to ask more when a familiar voice cooing about the dogs came barreling down the hallway and walked right into the room.

"Hi there, Caspar!"

I didn't remember telling her my name, but what threw me off was the way she floated into the room as though she was propelled by joy. It was like this woman was the sun in this building, and even the golden retriever who dropped a tennis ball at my feet looked at me like, *"yeah, I know, I'm not nearly as interesting or fun as she is, I'm just here for the belly rubs, man."*

I patted the dog on the head and glanced up at her, she was wearing a yellow floral dress that floated at her ankles, ID badge and lanyard draped around her neck, and about fifty bracelets on her wrists, each beaded no doubt by someone she knew. Her curly hair was pulled up into a bun at the nape of her neck, and a white bandana held the frizzy flyaways out of her line of sight. She had emerald green eyes, I noticed.

"I thought you said I missed the dogs," I said to Ansa.

"You got lucky I guess," she muttered to me and smiled at Tessa.

"This is Charlie," she said, patting the dog on his head, "he is just leaving now, but I guess he sniffed someone he didn't get to say hello to this morning and came right for you, friendly ghost!"

I shot Ansa a glare, and she put her hands up as if to claim innocence until proven guilty.

"Will we see you guys today at Jazz-ercise?"

To my horror, Ansa nodded excitedly.

"Excellent! Come on Charlie, we can't make dad wait all day, buddy!" And with that, she was gone. I wondered if everyone saw her as a shooting star. She was someone you saw for just a flash of time, but her presence lingered in the room long after she had gone. Even Ansa looked less sunken in her wheelchair, her complexion looking brighter too after the visitor bounded away, talking to herself and the dog all the way down the hallway.

"You were saying something about a bird you saw?"

I had entirely forgotten.

"Beautiful," I murmured, half to myself, still staring at the empty doorway where Tessa had stood.

"Yeah, that's love," a small voice said behind me.

I was about to give her a hard time and out-right refuse the suggestion being made. She looked as though she would cry though, so I quickly asked her about her morning and how she slept. We spent the rest of the morning telling each other about our families.

She told me more of Elena, her daughter.

"She was so confident, and I think that scared me. I was scared she would fly too high and get lost. I held her back a lot I think, told her the world had limits that we had to operate within. Told her some people were luckier than others, and that was the only differentiator. I watched her struggle with what I was trying to teach her, and I cringe at remembering the lights in her eyes dim as I tried to stomp it out entirely. I hope she knows all I wanted to do was protect her from life hurting her.

"I get it now though; I get why they say everything changes on your deathbed. How I wish I could go back in time and tell her to fly as high as she damn-well pleased because one day an accident would be all it takes to wipe her existence away. I wish I told her she could cure all the diseases of the world, that she could cure humanity even. I wish I could go back and really truly believe in her—I wish I could tell her how utterly proud I was of that conviction in her eyes, of the fire in her heart that burned for others. I wish I could tell her to hang onto that innocent child inside of you who believes they can walk on the moon simply if they will it to be. Because she deserved to know the world is not such a cruel place if you don't let it be.

"I wish more than anything else, that I had told her more of how much I loved her. I wish I had told her to love more, to love freely and openly and vastly because love is the only thing that matters at the end.

"Of course, I wish it had been me in that car on that day last year. Of course. But regardless, what upsets me more is that she may have died feeling as though she was nothing more than a small speck atop the earth, and that was my doing. I wanted for so long after the accident to simply have ten minutes with her, to tell her of all the things she could do, and I believed she could do them all because she was infinitely brighter than I could have ever imagined.

"She was like my husband, you know, so much more like him than me. He always built her up, he paid for any education she wanted and told her she would do the impossible, and I always told him he was setting her up for failure so young, that she needed to follow the order of things, that she needed to find a husband and have children. I couldn't see what he saw for so long, and when I did realize, it was too late. It is too late for me, Caspar."

I shook my head at her, refusing to believe that these were confessions of a dying woman. She took my hands in her mine, resting them atop her lap in the wheelchair; she was so cold I had to fight the urge to pull away. She clenched my hands in her tiny fists.

"But you—you have so much time. And I want you to know how utterly infinite you are. I want to tell you all those things I didn't get to tell Elena, because I see her spirit in you, and I knew when I saw you a few nights ago, I knew I had to at least try to get you to see yourself."

I sat back in my chair and digested all her words, only slightly registering the steady stream of tears falling down my cheeks.

"Stop your crying boy, we've got a jazz-ercise class to get to." She pointed to a small clock hanging on the wall in the tiny room. At least it was a single bedroom, no noisy neighbours or anything. Her room was simple, yellow faded walls with chipped paint. A standard hospital bed, with knitted blankets added by Ansa. She had a few stuffed animals resting on her bedside table.

I groaned at the thought of whatever jazz-ercise would entail, but the smile on the woman's face and the kind words she had offered moments earlier had me rolling her through the hallways, ready to take on whatever Tessa had planned for the afternoon.

I was not upset at the thought of seeing those emerald eyes again, either.

.

CHAPTER NINE

Tessa

I always loved pet therapy days. When I was sick, I remembered the days the golden retriever, Buddy, would jump onto my bed and nudge my hands. Even on the toughest days, the days I only remember my mom and dad watching me in horror, watching their only daughter fade away before their very eyes.

I remembered watching as Buddy would sit between their knees and nuzzle his furry head against their ankles. He became family, in the same way I now got to bring Charlie into my patients' rooms. The difference was, Charlie was my own—an adopted best friend, who joined my home with my parents just shy of six years ago. My dad brought him home one night, and I think we all knew who he reminded us of.

Charlie ran right for the red pickup truck as soon as I swung open the doors. My dad swung the passenger seat door open, and Charlie hopped right in. Sometimes I expected dad to pull the seatbelt around him and throw a pair of sunglasses over his wet nose.

I waved at him, and he flashed a goofy grin, and like that they were gone.

My dad drove me to work on the days I would tour Charlie around, he would sit in the cab of his pickup truck and read the newspaper while he waited to get his favourite child, not me, back in the seat next to him. When we all drove in the truck together, I had to squish into the middle seat, with Charlie getting the passenger window because dad insisted, he 'needed the fresh air.'

I shook my head and smiled, closing the metal doors. I was very fortunate to have a great childhood, aside from the cancer. I had incredibly cool artist parents, who truly gave me all of themselves. They were meant to raise a family, and I think if mum could have had more kids, I would be overrun by siblings. Mom always said I was the best one hit wonder to ever hit Ireland though, so there was that I guess.

When dad found out I was saving money to move out, he was devastated. He took it worse than any mother, even the ones I've seen crying as they hug their child goodbye on the first day of Uni. Mum and I had to sit down with him and tell him about the importance of finding your way in the world, but even after he agreed that it was probably way past that time in my life, I saw the way he started to stare at me like I was that little girl with leukemia again.

He was just afraid of losing me, he was afraid that I would be gone forever. I had a lot of patience though because I know what they went through those eight months may very well have been worse than they were in my own memory.

On my way back to the floor, I stopped by the community inspiration wall and hung up the polaroid picture I had snapped of the supposedly too-grumpy-to-smile Marge, with Charlie from this morning.

She was grinning ear to ear in a way she had never smiled when I went to talk with her. Sometimes animals just comforted better. I smiled at the picture while letting myself enjoy the moment. It was great to get people to laugh and smile but getting that person who seemed so far away from reality to feel something positive… that was why I did this job and why I loved every single moment of it.

I hopped to the nursing station and took attendance from this morning's walk around with Charlie. I documented about Marge, and added not one, but two exclamation marks. I knew everyone would share my enthusiasm and stop by the inspiration wall on their next rotation.

By the time emails were checked, coffee was consumed, a few morning prayers were said, and quiet bedside reading, it was time for lunch.

I didn't have an office; the little lounge at the back of the unit was where I hoarded my programming supplies. It was what Lorraine liked to refer to as the organized disaster of the floor. Only I knew the exact science of squeezing four supply closets worth of stuff into a room without it looking like it had been overtaken by raccoons.

Herb had called and asked if he could join me for lunch, I swung by his room on the way and transferred him into his wheelchair.

"What's on the menu today, Tess?"

"For you my kind friend, the highest quality Shepherd's pie, served with a side of small talk and maybe even some medium talk if time permits."

He grinned over his shoulder at me and asked, "Gravy?"

"As if there was any other option!" I feigned horror at the thought.

We reached the lounge just as lunch trays were

rolling by with the friendly faced kitchen staff who were sliding trays into all the rooms. I made a mental note to see if we could have a diner day, where they wore roller skates and tutus and we put cardboard cut-outs of antique cars on the patient doorframes.

We. Had. To. Do. That.

"What did you just think about?" Herb asked, as I grabbed two trays from the trolley and slid them onto the table in the lounge.

"Oh, you'll see." I waggled my brows.

"Dear lord, help us all."

We had lunch and that small talk, he shuffled his food around more than anything else, which made my stomach churn. I knew he was one of the ones who would hide it and told myself to treasure the moment even more.

"Knock, knock," I teased.

"Who's there?"

"Tank."

"Tank who?"

"Herb, you don't have to thank me for eating lunch with you," I offered, scooping potatoes onto my fork.

Laughter echoed the halls, and I smiled even though I knew how soon I would be missing that laugh.

"Do you think they will remember me?"

I knew he meant his grandchildren; they had been estranged over some silly fight him and his son had gotten into years ago, I didn't know details, I never really needed to know details. They offered what they wanted; I didn't pry. I wanted them to be in control of as much as they could be in these days where the situation at hand seemed so out of control.

I shrugged. "I think they will remember the small things, maybe the crook of your nose, or your broken glasses."

"Is that what you will remember?" Herb asked in a serious tone, watching me move my food around the plate.

"I will remember you, if that's what you're asking."

"How, though?"

I looked at him with a pained expression, I had known him the longest out of everyone on the floor now. It was hard, every day was hard. But these moments, they made you question if you were mentally sane for choosing to get up and come here every day. Not many other careers involved growing connections with people only to helplessly watch them cease to exist in front of your own eyes.

"I'll remember that damned sweater," I gestured to the green hooded sweatshirt, with a leprechaun in a fighting stance, his favourite one that no one could tell me when it had been last washed, "and the smell of it."

He laughed, but the serious tone was not fading from the room, and I knew he was waiting for a truthful answer.

"I'll remember the way your eyes crinkle at

the edge when you smile." I could feel the colour draining from my face. "I'll remember the sound of your laugh."

He had a beautiful smile on his face. "I'll most certainly remember your love of all things Neil Diamond and how hard you try to pretend you are 'indifferent' to Taylor Swift, when you are clearly madly in love."

He laughed at that one, and I noticed his hand holding his chest. He was in pain.

"But most of all, I'll remember you as you are. Not as your mistakes, not as the strained relationship with your son. I'll remember the man who still asks about my parents, the one who knows when I am having a bad day. Herb, I could never forget anything about you, my friend."

I drew in a shaky breath, and I know he heard how hard this was.

He outstretched a palm on the table. "Would you call my son for me?"

My brows arched. "Yes. Why?"

"I want to meet my grandchildren, and I fear I don't have as long as we had thought, my dear fire-headed friend."

I nodded and went for the phone on the wall.

"Tessa," he called, "I hope I get to remember you too."

His son and I spoke a few words; he didn't have to ask how urgent it was, I assumed he could hear it in my voice, because he promptly told me he would be there with the kids by dinner time. I brought Herb back to his room and asked him if he wanted to come to jazz class, even though I knew the answer. Before I went to tell Lorraine, I grabbed my cellphone from the metal cabinet where I stored my raincoat, boots, and purse during the day.

You: Hey, I'll be late tonight.

Old Man: Everything alright?

You: Yeah... I will call when ready.

Old Man: Okay, love you.

You: Love you too, Dad.

I told Lorraine, and she asked if she should set up the cot. I told her that was a good idea. It was going to be a rough night, and I knew the energy on the floor had changed in just a few moments. We were quite the synchronized group of people, and when it was a day like today—we just knew.

When I started setting up chairs in the main foyer, since we didn't have enough room in the lounge for a proper jazz-ercise group, I felt the air go out of the floor. We all watched the maintenance folks roll a cot into the room and knew. The nurse who was crushing medications, started to sniffle and someone else jumped in with a reassuring shoulder squeeze so she could go get some air. We had each other's backs, and that was such a valuable thing. We were all family here, really and truly.

I counted four deep breaths and willed a smile to come. It did, and I brushed off the hems of my dress and started to gather my friends from their rooms. I saw the oddball Caspar and his grandmother making their way down the hallway and smiled as he met my eyes.

His grandmother waved at me, her tiny pink glasses looking brighter than yesterday.

"Do you shine those spectacles of yours, Ansa?"

"With only the best shoeshine!"

The grandson shifted his weight between his legs awkwardly, as I caught him staring at me again, and wondered if I had shepherd's pie on my face.

"Have you had the chance to see our community inspiration board yet? Feel free to add anything, it is as much your home as it is everyone else's."

"We will be sure to swing by." Caspar motioned to the board and smiled at me, which did not go missed by his grandmother. I watched her eyebrows shoot so high up they may have left her face.

I nearly snorted in laughter, what a strange pairing these two were. I watched Caspar bring his grandmother to the edge of the group and watched the distance he stayed from her. I wondered what their stories were, as they certainly did not behave as grandson and grandmother. He looked at her like she was both a stranger and a friend from long ago, connected in some distant way.

I found myself distracted during the class, watching the way Ansa and Caspar interacted and spoke in hushed tones, and Herb's absence, with my eyes continually drifting to the space he usually occupied. I watched the doctor go into his room, followed by Lorraine, and I watched as she shook her head at me. I felt my heart do a belly flop against my diaphragm.

It was hard to finish the class, but I tried to focus on Marge and the way she scolded other people for being too loud or moving too slowly. I tried to laugh, but I had never faked anything about myself in these walls.

We ended the class with impromptu meditation.

"Deep breath in, and when you breathe out—

let go.

Breathe in courage—breathe out fear.

Breathe in resiliency—breathe out pain.

Breathe in love—let go of all your sorrow."

I watched Lorraine place a tea candle in a mason jar and leave it on the small shelf outside of Herb's room.

"Breathe in hope—and let go of worry."

It was bound to be a long evening.

CHAPTER TEN

Ansa

Tessa was acting differently. I watched her try to maintain composure while the staff flew in and out of one of my neighbours' rooms. She greeted the patients, but not with her usual skip in her step and smile that lit up the room. She was sunken in on herself. I wondered how many others noticed.

"Do you want to go back to your room?" Caspar grew more uncomfortable, as he was realizing what was happening to the poor man who had sat next to us the other night, and I remembered learning that his name was Herb when we had played that game of balloon badminton. A German name, one often being the short form version of Herbert. It vaguely translated to "Illustrious Warrior". I hoped he would find peace at the end of his battle.

The charge nurse put a small tea candle outside of his room, and I thought about the same shelf sitting empty outside of my room we had just come from.

"No," I shrugged, "I know where I am."

He asked me about four other times in the span of the next half hour of our exercise class. I was beginning to think Tessa would ask us to sit in the back of the classroom for interrupting, with all our hushed conversations. But she was so focused on trying not to cry, hardly looking away from the tea candle.

When the class was over, she was gone before anyone could chat with her. I watched her disappear into the washroom, and noticed I was not the only one watching her.

He chewed on his lower lip. "Doesn't it scare the shit out of you?"

I smirked at him, lowered my voice a few octaves and served a dose of his own medicine, "Not nearly as much as living does."

He rolled his eyes at me, and I realized just how much I liked this young man, and how very much like my Elena he was. He pushed me back to my room, the sun starting to set behind my window.

"Do you think she's okay?" Caspar asked.

"Working here, I'm sure everyone has their own ways to take care of themselves."

He stared at me with a question on his face; I wished I could just hear what he was thinking.

"Have you always kept your hair long?" I asked, as he helped me into bed wrapping an arm around my waist.

"Yeah, I used to get teased a lot for it and almost cut it off after one year of grade school, but my mom stopped me."

"I told you about my Elena, when do I get to hear of your darling Aiyana?"

He looked at me strangely, and I wondered if he was contemplating leaving, but then he sat in the reclining blue plastic chair beside me.

"What do you want to know?" he asked.

"What would she say to the man I met a few nights ago in the emergency room?"

His spine straightened, and I braced for an explosion, but he stayed still.

"I'm sorry if I overstepped," I said after a few minutes of silence had passed, and Caspar stared straight through me.

"No, it's okay," he said.

"I'm sure you have your reasons; I didn't mean to diminish that. I just don't understand why you would leave so early."

He shook his head, his long hair covering half of his gaze.

"She was the sun in my sky, and without her it's just so cold."

I nodded, knowing there was more but not

wanting to press him for information. He felt so familiar that it was hard not to lecture him about how important he was to the world. I wanted to scoop him into a hug and tell him all those things I had said earlier about my darling daughter.

"I took you on your cigarette endeavor last night, tonight it's my turn to choose where we go."

I pointed at him. "I like this game. But first, dinner."

He nodded in agreement. "What do you think is on the menu this evening?"

"I was hoping you would order us a pizza."

"Is this another bucket list item?"

"I can't leave the world without having another slice of cheese from that place on Lainey Drive," I said, shrugging.

"That's my favourite place too," he said and smiled, "I'll go pick it up, it'll be quicker."

We scribbled on a napkin what we wanted, and I gave him a twenty-dollar bill before he left.

I smiled, watching him through the window as he waited for a taxi, and remembered the last time I had that greasy mess from that restaurant. It was absolutely horrendous, but our Elena loved it. I told her countless times how unhealthy it was, and I refused to order it when she was in high school, telling her instead to ask her father to contribute to an increase in our family cholesterol. I preferred traditional home-cooked Indian cuisine, and some Irish favourites that had made their way into my recipe books.

I laughed and put my face in my hands. How fleeting life was! How silly I had been for so long, to think the small things were anything more than small. I was terribly jealous of my husband, of the small things he shared with her. The nights they would go out together for food and would ask me to come along. I was too stubborn, so I had missed out on those memories with them.

I only hoped I would get the chance to tell them that I understood now, I would eat in all the greasy pizza spots in the afterlife, take all the chances and risks, just to share those smiles and moments with my family.

I pulled the blanket up to my chin and felt so incredibly tired. In a matter of minutes, I found myself surrendering to sleep and dreaming about Caspar's mother. In my dream, she was with my family, they were sitting at a table laughing together. I approached, running and hugging Elena as soon as I could.

I watched the woman with braided hair mouth the words, *Thank you.*

And then I woke up to the smell of cheese, Caspar was seated in the same blue chair at my bedside, mid-bite with a slice of pizza.

He smiled, and waved a hand towards the box of pizza. "I'm sorry, the smell made me so hungry, but I didn't want to wake you up."

I propped myself up in bed and must have moved too quickly because the room spun around a few times, and I leaned my head back against the cold pillow.

"Are you okay?" he asked.

I nodded, but he knew it was a lie.

"Do you want me to get you a slice?"

We ate the whole pizza, and I was surprised at how much I enjoyed the taste. I wondered if it was the medication pumping through my veins, or the sweet memory of my daughter with the tomato sauce on her face when she was a kid. It warmed me from the inside.

We turned the television on and sat in silence for a few moments.

"Do you want me to stay?" he asked suddenly, pointing to something by the door.

They must have brought the cot in the room while I had been napping, but I shrugged at the question. "That's up to you, grandson."

He laughed and patted my knee through the blanket.

"You know you don't have to be here, right?" I offered.

"Of course. To be honest, I'm still not really sure why I am."

He looked down at his feet then, and I stayed silent. I think sometimes, silence speaks louder than words. I didn't have all the answers, there were only the things I knew so far and the things I may never know.

The sun had disappeared, when he helped me into my wheelchair, and we embarked on another evening expedition. This time, the journey was short.

We had found our way back in the hospital, the large empty foyer that had food court stalls, gift shops, and administration desks. It had been full the other night, when the paramedics had ushered me out of my room at the long-term care home I had moved into, and into this new short-stay home.

My final home.

It was small, but the emptiness made it feel

massive. Where there was usually a bustle of people milling about, there was silence. The music no longer drawled from the overhead speakers, and the PA system was not sounding off alarms or codes. It was peaceful, as we walked around a few times looking in the gift shop windows.

We ended up laughing about the irony of two cards sitting next to each other, one for a congratulations on having a baby, and the saying sorry for your loss. How curious was it that there were babies taking their first breaths somewhere in these walls, and new mothers cooing over the gurgles coming from their fuzzy headed additions? Even more curious, was the proximity of these new lives being down the hall from mourning widows, weeping children, and silent prayers.

This place held all the first and last breaths. Caspar shivered, despite it being warm inside and the thick hooded sweatshirt he wore. He rolled me over to the piano that was surrounded by fake greenery in the middle of the foyer.

I put the brakes on my wheelchair, and he sat on the wooden piano bench. I watched the way he lovingly lifted the cover from the keys and traced his fingers over the keys. His one hand, the one with the jagged scar, rested on top of his knee and twitched.

"My mother taught me how to play, we started learning when I was four. She would put her hands over mine and tell me to feel the music. I hated it at first, I didn't understand it at all, didn't understand why she pushed it on me even when I so clearly was not meant to be musically inclined. She never gave up; she would just tell me to start again and really feel the music come from my heart and pour over the piano. We spent years working on the basics, she would tell me it was in my blood. That her mother played for her, and her mother's mother taught her as well.

"By the time I was ten, I was competing. We would travel on the weekends; my mom would tie my hair back and straighten my bowtie. She would stand in the crowd and film every moment of every show. She always told me I was superb, even when I came in last in a lot of the early ones. I practiced, and I got better and by the time I was in high school I had music schools offering me scholarships. It was like a dream come true—for both of us. I saw how happy it made her, and I felt like I was taking care of both of us. I had always wanted to be able to take care of her, especially since for so long it was just her taking care of me. She lost my dad before I was born, she did it all on her own.

"I was in grad school; I was doing so well, and my music was starting to build a career. Professors were starting to ask me to help them outside of class, on their own shows and pieces. And then one day it was all gone. She was gone. Ironically, we were on the way home from a competition, which I won. I had a talent scout come up to me after the show finding out if I had any contracts on the go, and who left me with a business card and a promise of success. Mum insisted we drive home together, so she could treat me to ice-cream before dropping me off at my dorm to celebrate. She complained ever since qualifying for grad school, and really starting to take things seriously, we didn't spend enough time together anymore. As if that wasn't enough, the doctors said I may never regain the same level of functioning in my wrist. I have permanent nerve damage, and when I try to play… all I hear is failure."

He closed the lid on the keys and looked at me with such deep sadness in his eyes.

"I can only hear the music and see her face when I go to that place, and sometimes I want to stay there forever."

I stayed silent, but reached out my hand and placed it on his shoulder.

He cried for a few moments; ugly tears that were combined with shakes that racked his body. When he cried, I swear I could hear the music playing again through the overhead speakers.

Before we went back to the room, I broke the silence.

"Play something for me," I pleaded. "Anything."

His eyes were glossy and red, he looked at the piano and then back to me. "I can't."

I shook my head. "Yes, you can."

I had no idea how to play the piano, in fact I was not sure I could even reach both sides of the keys. I hauled myself from my chair onto the cold wooden bench and took his good hand in mine.

I placed our hands over the keys and waited. He slowly drawled his hand over the keys, taking mine with him. The sounds were hollow in the most beautiful way; I knew it didn't sound as it would have before his injury, but I still saw the beauty in it. And what's more, I knew he could hear it for himself. I didn't need to know his whole story, all I needed was to help him see his own future and what opportunities lie therein.

I thought about my family while my hand floated over the keys, on top of his. I wished I had learned to play an instrument with Elena.

We stayed like that for an hour before he stopped and looked at me. There was such a story written in those eyes, such a life meant to be lived. I hoped I could help him somehow continue to try when he had such a passionate and kind heart. The world needed more people like him in it, more people who just wanted to make music and hold hands with the dying. I knew he was broken, but in that moment, he seemed more whole than anyone I had ever crossed paths with.

He looked just like his mother had when I saw her in my dreams this afternoon, as he mouthed the words *thank you* in my direction. I smiled back.

As we walked back to the unit, my final resting place, he hummed the song. It was beautiful, perhaps the most beautiful song I had ever heard.

It reminded me of summer back home, and I found my eyes closing against my will. Again, a feeling of overwhelming urgency to let my eyes close and surrender to sleep overcame me.

When I woke up, the first thing I noticed was how many stars were in the night sky, and the second thing I noticed was the steady snoring from the floor beside me, where Caspar laid tucked under hospital sheets on the small cot.

I smiled and hoped I had the chance to thank his mother as well, for raising someone with such empathy and kindness to keep a dying woman company.

CHAPTER ELEVEN

Tessa

I sat in the bathroom and cried, the kind of crying where everyone would be able to see it on my face. I had barely gotten through teaching that exercise class before the tears burst through the mental dam I had tried to put up.

I splashed cold water on my face, hoping it would reduce my swollen eyes, before heading back to the nurse's station to join the rest of the team for afternoon rounds. We went through any updates on patients, and when we got to Herb, the room went quiet.

"Will it be tonight?" An oncoming shift nurse asked. Lorraine nodded.

"Looks that way."

I spotted a man through the glass window, holding hands with two kids who had fiery red hair. I nudged Lorraine and jerked my chin towards where they stood. She excused herself from rounds, and I watched as she led the family to Herbs room.

The nurses chatted for a while, sharing memories they had of Herb while he had been a part of our little family the past year. We laughed and cried openly, letting ourselves grieve and heal simultaneously.

When we all went our separate ways, I headed to the lounge at the back of the unit. I decided to put together two pink folders worth of colouring pages, crayons, and stickers. As I was putting together the folders, I heard laughter echo down the hallway and peered my head around the corner. It was Caspar and his grandmother, as they balanced boxes of pizza on her lap and strolled down the hallway. They both had such genuine happiness on their faces, and

I returned to making the folders with a smile on my own face as well.

"Tessa, do you have a moment?" A familiar voice from the doorway called to me, I spun around to see a stout woman with bobbed black hair.

I sighed, knowing what she wanted to talk about.

"Come on in, Mrs. Drew." I waved at the empty chair across from where I was making folders.

"I sent a few emails," she said. I nodded. "I was wondering what your thoughts are."

"Well, I would rather dislike having to re-sign," I replied flatly.

She sighed, and I felt bad instantly. It wasn't her fault that the hospital board was cutting my job, it was all about the financials and budget plans.

"If you resign, I can offer you a package, and you at least have something to get you through until we can get you back. I will fight for your job, Tessa."

She was a kind woman, but it was hard to

forgive the messenger. They first told me about the budget cuts about a year ago. Initially it was only reduced hours, and then I got notice my entire position would be lost in the new fiscal year, but that the responsibilities of the role would be upheld by the physiotherapy team. Don't get me wrong, the physio ladies were amazing, but they were focused primarily on the physical rehabilitation aspect, whereas I advocated for the mental healing. I pushed back at first and was told they would listen to me and ensure I would find a position on another team in the hospital.

"You can't make any guarantees though, right?"

"I will try another pitch in six months, but if we delay your resignation anymore, we will lose any chance at it."

Her eyes were pleading; I knew she was telling the truth.

"What are they offering?"

She shuffled the papers she had in her hands

and slid them across the top of the table towards me.

"Your last day would be in about a month. Then you would join the administration team on a part time basis for a temporary time and you would be paid out six months' salary. Meanwhile, you and I will work on a pitch; I already have confirmation they will hear our arguments again and revisit the budget for the role."

She looked at me expectantly.

"Can I think on it?"

"Of course, but not for long unfortunately— they are really on me about it. I'll leave it with you for the week though. Please, consider it. If you try to fight it, I can't help much. It's out of my hands."

I nodded solemnly and tucked a few strands of hair behind my ear. I wasn't worried about the money; I was worried about losing myself. This job, these people in these walls had saved me once, and I think every day since then too. I was meant to be here. Without that, I was not sure who I would be.

We chatted a bit longer, before my boss excused herself and asked if I was working a night shift. I told her about Herb, and she smiled at me and patted my shoulder before mumbling apologies and promptly leaving.

I think the topic of death really makes some people uncomfortable, Mrs. Drew included. It makes the usual steady stream of words coming out of their mouths turn into a white-water rafting experience, and you can see them struggle to maintain composure, and panic. I was thankful in this situation, as I was ready to simply say I would do my job on a volunteer basis. I had to think about my future though. I bit my lip and continued to put stickers on the pink folders.

I forgot the exchange I had with Mrs. Drew entirely as I walked down the hallway towards the room with the candle perched beside the door. I passed Ansa and her grandson again, just coming back to her room with the boxes of pizza still on her lap. They offered a wave, and I swore I saw red flood Caspar's cheeks when he smiled shyly at me. I told myself tomorrow I needed to get to know the dynamic duo better.

But for now, I was standing in the doorway watching as Herb told his granddaughters knock-knock jokes.

"I hope I'm not interrupting," I said.

They all looked my way as I quickly placed the two pink folders in front of the little girls with hair just like mine.

"I made some activities for you little ladies to work on while you visit my friend here."

"McKenzie and Rose, this is my friend Tessa—the one who always has the best adventures."

His son looked as if someone had told him the world was about to fall out of the sky. Years of pain were etched on his face, and I watched him look at me and then look away with tears brimming his eyes. The two young girls, however, were oblivious to their surroundings, keeping a youthful innocence presence in the room.

I sat on the floor with Herb's granddaughters for a while, trying not to eavesdrop on the extremely intimate conversation between a dying man and his estranged son.

We coloured as I told them stories about me and their grandfather, about our journeys together to the great garden outside, to the day we went on a trip on our bus to the ice-cream shoppe down the street. They asked the best questions, some of them serious and some of them making me fight back laughter.

"What flavour ice-cream did Grandpa order?" the younger one, Rose asked.

"Plain vanilla." I smiled at her.

"That's my favourite too, do you think that was genetic?"

I furrowed my eyebrows and put a pencil to my chin. "I think you may be right! I will have to consult with a doctor though, but I will let you know."

"When did Grandpa get those lines on his face?" the older one, McKenzie, was staring at her dad and grandfather as she asked the question.

"When you start to grow up, after a lot of years and time you start to get them. They're called wrinkles."

"Is Grandpa going to be okay?" Rose asked.

"Yes. He's just not going to be with us here on earth much longer," I said, holding their gazes.

"Is Grandpa going to die?" McKenzie looked at me as she asked, and I knew she needed the truth. I think sometimes we shield kids from that truth out of love, and from not wanting to disrupt their innocence. But sometimes that makes it more difficult. And sometimes, I think we underestimate kids and their intelligence.

"Yes. It's okay to be sad about that, but it won't hurt him, and when we miss him, we can talk to him in our heads." I tapped my own head for emphasis.

"Does Grandpa have a name?" Rose asked.

"Herbert, but he lets his friends call him Herb." I watched as she wrote To: Herb on her colouring page.

"Will daddy be sad forever?" asked McKenzie, as she stared at her dad.

"No, but it will take some time for daddy to be happy again. He will just be missing Grandpa, but he is lucky to have you two to keep him smiling."

"I'm sad," McKenzie said, and Rose reached her hand out to hold her sister's.

"That's okay. What's important is that you know how much your grandpa, and your family loves you," I said.

We stayed like that for a few hours; Herb and his son talking through what they needed to, the girls and I colouring. I took the girls to the cafeteria at one point for a snack, and on our way back we heard music flooding the hallway. Rose wanted to follow the music, and when we did, we wound up in the main lobby. We walked to the main doors to see who else but our dynamic duo, Caspar and Ansa, seated at the piano. It looked as though Ansa was teaching him how to play, but she was so small next to his broad shoulders I could only see her tiny hands resting on his.

"Can we go closer?" Rose tugged on my hand.

"Let's head back to see grandpa, your dad will think we have had more than our fill of chocolate puddings!" I smiled, half at them and half at the two figures playing the piano in front of us, oblivious to us standing by the doors. We turned and walked back to the unit, slower than I had ever gone before. I wanted to keep listening to the sound of the song being reflected on the soft walls that were void of sound otherwise. It was always so eerily quiet in a small-town hospital at nighttime, as we did not have the normal hustle and bustle of a city hospital.

When we got back to the unit, Herb's son was standing at the nurse's station, his face in his hands. I cleared my throat and watched as he gained enough composure to smile at his daughters.

"We gotta get you little ladies home or Mum will kill me, come say goodbye to Grandpa before we leave."

He nodded at me in thanks as the girls grabbed his hands and followed him into the room.

I let them have some privacy and ate my late-night dinner in the nurse's station, watching the odd-ball Caspar and Ansa return to the floor. I couldn't help but notice he had been here all day. I grabbed her chart from a nearby cabinet and flipped through it. There was no mention of any grandsons, it only said widowed and lost a daughter. Her power of attorney was through the government, not a relative. There was more to that story, and I was determined to find out the mysterious surrounding it. I still remembered when Caspar bumped into me a few short days ago and seemed like he was caught doing something illegal. Now, he seemed at home beside Ansa.

Her prognosis was not good, and there was something I had not known: Ansa was being seen by our Medical Assistance in Dying team and was scheduled to leave the world on August 15th, if she had not passed naturally before then. I wondered if her grandson knew, since it did not seem that way.

In my time here, I had only worked with two people who opted for medically assisted deaths, and they were both surrounded by family in the weeks before.

Ansa, though. She was different.

My attention shifted when I heard Herb's son let Lorraine know he was leaving and thanked her for everything. I walked out of the nurse's station and waved at him just as the girls were bounding out of the room and towards us.

We exchanged a knowing look, then he was gone along with the glowing spirits of Herb's granddaughters. Lorraine gave my shoulder a squeeze.

"Are you going to stay?" she asked.

"Yeah, how is he?"

"Won't be long now; he is having a hard time catching his breath."

"Okay." I looked at the candle flickering in his doorway. "Are you staying too?"

She nodded. "I'll be here for afterwards, I said goodbye though. Let me know if you guys need anything, I am right out here."

I smiled and nodded, going into the bathroom to change into trackpants and a hooded sweatshirt. The sweatshirt was still a bright shade of pink, and the trackpants were a lighter shade of pink. I refused to let death take away colour.

Before I walked to his room, I took a few deep breaths, preparing myself.

He smiled as I walked over and sat on the cot next to his bed, which had been lowered close to the floor so he wouldn't fall.

"I was hoping I would get to spend my final moments with such a ray of sunshine at my side," he laughed. Tears stung my eyes as I reached out and grasped his hand.

146

CHAPTER TWELVE

Tessa

My favourite poet Ralph Waldo Emerson once said, "What lies behind you, and what lies in front of you, pales in comparison to what lies inside of you."

Herb held my hand tightly in his, wincing in pain but waving his hand away when I reached for the call bell.

"Last night, I was on the internet." He laughed, and I joined.

"Oh boy, here we go."

He shushed me and went on, "I was trying to think of something badass to say right before it happens, y'know?"

I shook my head at him, still smiling.

"So many good ones are already taken. Some of them so ridiculously clever. There was a French guy who studied grammar, he said, 'I am about to, or I am going to—die: Either expression is correct.' Can you imagine the laughter that would have been heard when he said that and then croaked?"

We laughed at the absurdity.

"Last words are for the fool who hasn't said enough," I quoted, waggling my eyebrows.

"Karl Marx!" he laughed, "So you have researched these as well."

He started to cough, a violent sound. He was red in the face before he caught a shaky inhale.

"Do you need anything, Herb?"

"I have everything I could have ever asked for; I was a miserable son of a gun most of my life. I took people for granted, I used people, I burned bridges and wondered why I was alone for so many years."

I waited for him to continue, through another

fit of coughs and deeply jagged breaths.

"But tonight, I got to say sorry to the people who mattered most. My son deserved a better father. He is a better man than I ever was and being able to see him and hear his voice again… It was all I could have imagined. And those girls of his, they will do wonders, don't you think?"

I nodded my head; he was pale as the moonlight that strayed into the room. I could see he was struggling to keep his eyes open now, and his chest and abdomen were slow to rise with each breath.

"They have the same kind of wit that their grandfather has, and a good sense of humour," I said, squeezing his hand.

"You know, without you I don't know if I would have gotten to meet those girls. You're the one who helped me call him, you were there every step of the way. Why did you help me?"

"It's what I do, Herb."

He shook his head and used all the strength

he had to turn over and look me straight in the eyes.

"No way, girl, that's not it. That may be it for some people, but not for you."

"What do you mean?" I asked, emotions welling up in my chest.

"This isn't a job to you; it's not what you do, it's who you are. You are a gift to this world, never let anyone tell you otherwise."

I didn't have the heart to tell him about the conversation I had with Mrs. Drew earlier, but I felt like he knew. When news first spread through the floor about my job coming up to the chopping block, a lot of my patients tried to fight for me. Herb was a force to be reckoned with. He marched straight down to Mrs. Drews office and demanded that it be reconsidered. They had bought me more time, but that borrowed time was running short.

"You have to keep being yourself, Tessa, the world needs you," he said, seeing the look in my face. "People like me, miserable old folks who don't have anyone around and feel scared, we need someone like you to open the curtains and let some light in when it's getting too dark."

He gave me that intense stare again. "Promise me something?"

I nodded, and tilted my head, waiting.

"Promise me you'll name your firstborn child after me."

We both burst out into laughter. Lorraine popped her head in, a smile on her face. I patted the spot next to me on the cot and she joined us. Herb took her hand in his other one and closed his eyes.

"Promise me," he said, looking between me and Lorraine, "promise me that you will keep true to who your heart tells you to be. Ignore everything else, that's where I went wrong. I listened to the pressures of the world, instead of just listening to my heart. Nothing else matters when you are here, not a damned thing can come with you. So just, just listen to what your heart wants at all costs."

We looked at each other, as Herb closed his eyes.

"I am gay."

Both of us thought we had misheard him, but he said it over and over again. Those three words became a mantra.

"I am gay, I am gay, I am not heterosexual—I love men. I loved a man, a long time ago, when the world was much less accepting. I ran away from everything. I ran away from him. He wrote letters for years, I told my wife he was a friend from Belgium, and he told the same thing. I became a bitter, angry person because I let myself. It was nobody's fault except my own, and tonight I finally came out of that damned closet to my son. And now to you two as well. I am an openly gay man, and proud of who I am for the first time in my life. Sadly, I don't have long to revel in it or find men to take home to my parents, but maybe I will get into gay heaven."

We laughed, all three of us. We dubbed the

evening a deathbed coming out party. Lorraine stayed with us and called the cafeteria and had them bring us a Jell-O cup of every colour possible. One of the nurses put them all in a cup and we had pride Jell-O together.

We shared laughs and everyone told him how happy they were for him. It was a beautiful moment to bear witness to. After the midnight snack had finished, it was silence as Lorraine and I sat at his bedside and listened to the changes in his breathing.

It happened so fast. One moment he was breathing normally, the next a loud and sharp inhale.

In the early hours of the morning, Herb whispered, *"here I go"* as he took his last Earthside breath, surrounded by myself and Lorraine, each holding a hand. The doctor was there from the ER department within a few moments and checked for a pulse.

"Time of death, 1:33am," he pronounced. Lorraine went to call the morgue and his son.

I stayed with him, until a nurse came to take

him to the morgue.

His hand was still warm in mine, his face left in a permanent smile. I had his favourite green sweater in my lap, he had told me to keep it and to wear it when I get married so I know my husband isn't just in it for the looks. I snickered at the memory and let go of his hand.

I missed him as soon as he was gone, and Lorraine and I shared a hug before all the other nurses and unit staff gathered around and we shared a moment of silence.

Within a few moments, we had our jackets on and were saying our goodnights.

"Is your dad coming?" Lorraine asked, car keys dangling from her hands.

"Yeah, I just messaged him," I replied. "See you tomorrow."

I stared at the stars until my dad came to get me, and a damned shooting star came across the night sky just as the pickup truck rolled up. My dad stared at it through the windshield, and I smiled at him and Charlie.

I bounded over to the truck, and my dad stared at me like he had a question he wanted to say but was unsure how to put it into words. He waggled his brows, and tilted his head to the side, and I knew he was worried. I had seen that face many times before. I just leaned my head on his shoulder, and his kissed my curly red hair and wrapped an arm around my shoulders, Charlie resting his furry head in my lap.

Truth be told, we all knew Herb was a colourful soul, we just couldn't have imagined how darkened the world had made him. I felt like I had seen a rainbow explode in the middle of a long winter, in a person who I thought I had known.

Truth be told, I was so damn happy I was crying out of sheer joy.

Joy for him, for his courage to say those three words that had felt so unbearable all his life. I was so damn proud to have met such a vibrant life, even if I only understood its brilliance as an outsider looking in on a short glimpse of his life.

I smiled and thought about what the love of his life would say when they saw each other again. I smiled wider, thinking about the story they may write together in another time, in another life.

I believed in that kind of stuff; I had to. I had to believe there was more.

CHAPTER THIRTEEN

Caspar

I woke before Ansa.

I stared at the ceiling and wondered what I was thinking; the absurdity of everything happening was too much so I decided to go home and take a shower.

But when I got home, it felt empty. I found myself putting my shoes back on, my hair still wet from the shower and my laundry piling up in the corner of the tiny loft. As I grabbed my wallet off the counter, my eyes caught on the small photo of me and my mother at my high school graduation which was framed and sitting on top of the keyboard.

I walked through the loft and gently picked

up the photo off the hidden keyboard before putting it in my pocket, along with the bottle of pain pills, of which I had taken two before showering.

I thought my wrist would hurt more with the memory of playing the piano last night flickering over my brain. But it didn't, and I wasn't sure if that was real or if my mind was playing tricks on me. Regardless, I found myself back on the way to the hospital before I even had time to question why. I think in the back of my brain, somewhere remote, was my logic screaming at me that this entire scenario didn't make sense.

But I didn't need it to make sense, I just needed to follow the feeling of being alive. I had been fighting for that feeling for a while now and I wasn't about to let it slip away. This was probably the last chance I had at living; for some reason I felt as though Ansa and her pink glasses held the key to life, the key that would keep me from hurting myself.

On the way back to the hospital, I watched

the clouds and let my mind wander while I put one foot in front of the other.

Ansa had woken up while I was gone; she offered a small wave before picking up a slice of toast off her breakfast tray.

"Want some?" she asked, pushing the tray across the table towards the blue chair I lowered myself into.

"No thanks, I had some cereal at home."

She nodded, and we sat in silence most of the morning. There were no activities going on with Tessa, making the floor abnormally quiet. When lunch was nearing, she showed up in the doorway with an envelope.

"Good morning Ansa, Caspar." Her voice had shifted from the cheerfulness we were accustomed to. "How is the morning finding you both?"

Ansa smiled and pushed her glasses up the bridge of her nose.

"We've just been relaxing, and Caspar went

home to shower because he was starting to smell like dirty feet." She pinched her nose, and I shot her a glare.

"Oh dear! Well, I have to say I don't notice any bad odors lingering, so that's good." She winked at me, and I felt my heart race in my chest.

"We were just going to go for a walk in the garden," I said, desperate to change the subject as I felt my cheeks burn.

Ansa snickered.

"Well, funny you mention the garden because that's where we are all headed as well." Tessa smiled, but it didn't reach her eyes like normal.

"One of our friends passed away last night," she explained, "and we always have a little memorial service."

The air shifted in the room. I wondered if Ansa was thinking about her own memorial services.

"What time should we arrive?" Ansa asked, with no sign of discomfort noted on her face.

"We are all heading there now. I will see you both there," she said, nodding at us before she left.

"Are you sure?" I asked.

"Of course, besides I quite enjoy playing matchmaker between you and Tessa." She laughed at the look on my face.

"Yeah, well, telling people I smell like dirty feet isn't going to help me in the ladies department, my friend."

"Have you ever been in love?" she asked.

"How would I know?"

"Ah, so you haven't."

My brows furrowed and she added, "You will know. It will be like getting hit by a truck, but also skydiving into a vault of pillows."

I didn't say anything as we made our way outside. I noticed that the candle which was outside one of the rooms last night was gone, and inside the room there was a mattress without any sheets on it. The image sent shivers up my spine. I wanted to turn around and go back to the room, but Ansa reached up and put a hand on mine, and together we made our way out to the garden.

All the other patients were there, along with a group of staff that I had seen around the hallways but never formally met. The nurse who checked on Ansa throughout the night, who stepped over me on that uncomfortable cot, stood near the back of the group with Lorraine, their supervisor, the woman who was always at the nurse's station.

Tessa stood amongst the flowers, an image of beauty and grace, wearing a green sweater on with a leprechaun on it, and grey trackpants. Her hair was pulled back into a messy bun atop her head, but the strands of hair that frayed away seemed intentionally placed to frame her face. I honestly thought I had never seen a woman as beautiful as her.

It felt like skydiving just looking at her, and I had to remind myself where I was and instantly felt bad for thinking about how much I liked this woman at a time like this. Besides, she could be married for all I know. I instinctively checked for a ring and felt relief when I didn't see one. Then I went back to feeling absurd and trapped in a vicious cycle of my own thoughts.

"Are you sure you are okay being here?" I leaned down and asked Ansa, who was wrapped in a blanket and looked so tiny in her wheelchair. I swore she was shrinking every day.

She nodded her head and turned to look at me behind her. Her complexion looked paler today, and I wondered how long she had left.

"You don't have to stay if this kind of stuff bothers you," she said, and I knew what she was really saying. Did this make me want to take more pills and fall asleep forever? Truth be told, I had no idea what made me feel like that. I never sought any help; I only took the pills to feel something when I was in a valley of nothingness.

Strange as it may have seemed considering

the circumstances, I felt more alive there in that gar-den than I had since my mother passed away. I felt sadness, I felt anxiety.

But that was better than nothing.

The memorial service was quick but beauti-ful. Some of the other patients shared their memories of the gentleman we had met at balloon badminton the other day, which felt like ages ago. His name was Herb, he was born and raised Irish, and I came to find out that the sweater Tessa wore was his trademark sweater around the floor.

"Herb was an incredible person, he made us all laugh and he knew how to help us when we cried. He had a troubled past, but he had the chance to reconcile his truths at the end of his life in the most beautiful way, surrounded by family and friends. He feels no pain now, and his memory will live on with us and with his family, forever. We will remember him as the man in this sweater, as the man who heck-led us when we did singalongs, and simply as this man."

They played a slideshow of photos on a small projector screen near the flowerbeds, and memories floated over the crowd. There were sniffles, giggles, and a few outbursts of tears. When the stream of photos ended and the screen went black, Lorraine carried a small cage up to where Tessa was standing.

Tessa opened the door to the cage, and I watched in awe as twenty or thirty monarch butterflies flitted their way out into the soft afternoon breeze. One of them landed straight on Ansa's arm, and she looked at it with eyes wide and a big smile on her face. She closed her eyes and let out a heavy sigh, as the butterfly flew away towards the sky.

People slowly made their way back inside the building, Tessa lingering in the garden a while longer before making her way inside too. I could see tears running down her pale cheekbones. Ansa and I were the last two people outside in the garden, walking around the flowerbeds, saying nothing.

"Should we go get some lunch?" I asked.

"Caspar." Ansa looked up at me with a serious face. "I will be dead by the end of the summer."

CHAPTER FOURTEEN

Ansa

I watched as his face went through a flurry of emotions.

Shock, confusion, sorrow, anger—they all welled up behind his eyes. He sat on the bench next to me.

"I know I had told you I had a few weeks left to live in the emergency room," I continued, "but I didn't tell you why I was certain about it."

I explained everything to him, especially how chemotherapy had been exhausting. I told him about how I would be among the first of the Irish population to be considered for medical assistance in dying, about how hard people had fought to get that paperwork approved.

We chatted about the politics of it for a long while; I was passionate about being able to be an active participant in my own palliative care measures. I was passionate about being able to say when enough was enough, and when the pain became too much, I wanted to ensure I could pass with dignity.

"Is that why you first talked to me, you see this as a suicide of sorts?" Caspar asked.

"No, I told you why I talked to you already, friendly ghost. You perplex me, such a young and healthy man ready to leave all this behind." I waved to the garden around us, to the Earth as a whole.

"We all have our own lenses, Ansa." He pointed at my pink glasses resting on my nose.

I nodded. "Sorry, I didn't mean to offend."

"No offense taken; I just don't know why I'm here." He looked at me with sorrow in his eyes, genuine confusion tugging at his brows.

"Does anyone really know why they do anything?" I smiled at him, happy when he returned it. "Or do we all just make it up as we go along?"

We sat in the garden a few more moments, and the rest of the day moved in chunks:

We had lunch. We then vowed never to have the cafeteria hamburgers ever again, because they were more like hockey pucks.

Then we went to do a craft, and I watched the young man fumble his words around Tessa. It was like watching a puppy unsure how to walk, testing the waters by putting one paw in front of the other and then getting scared by its own shadow and deciding to just go for a nap instead.

Then dinner. Because of the hockey puck hamburgers, we opted to order from a local pizza parlour.

Medications, for myself from Lorraine, directly through the IV line in my arm, and for Caspar from the bottle he didn't think I saw him stuff into his pockets periodically.

And finally, rest.

At some point along the way, the order had to change to accommodate how utterly tired I began feeling.

Two weeks blurred together, and Caspar's stubble had turned into a small beard.

"I'm hoping to be back soon, but things are bad here. She is sleeping often, in a lot of pain." He was leaned against the window, resting his forehead against the glass, and a palm pressed against the countertop.

"I know, I'm sorry to leave you guys hanging but I have to be here for her." His breath fogged up the glass.

I wondered when he had gotten so good at lying for a moment before I realized he was not entirely hiding the truth. Sure, we weren't biologically connected in any way, but I was sleeping a lot and my time was drawing near. It was a new presence in the room, there ever since that day in the garden when there was an official date highlighted in the calendar of Caspar's mind.

His boss must have let him off the hook easy this morning; they had this exchange a few times a week. I felt bad for pulling him into this, I never wanted to disrupt his life as much as I had. I had only felt bad for the man in the hospital bed across from me who seemed as though he needed someone. I think a part of me had a morbid curiosity as well, since I was so close to deaths door—and this man had knocked on it several times.

I was terrified these days and started to withdraw a lot more. Caspar had taken to showering here too, so I was hardly ever alone. He knew how afraid I was, as he frequently caught me talking to the stars and pleading for my life to somehow be extended.

I almost called my lawyer yesterday to unravel everything we had worked to plan, everything I had worked so hard to ensure I would go from this world before I had to feel excruciating pain and become, for lack of a better term, a human vegetable.

I wanted dignity, but that didn't mean I had eliminated the quell of fear from the passage of time.

Tessa would eat takeout with us almost every night now, ever since I sent her a formal invitation one day by sliding her a card at our crafts class, telling her to join us that night. My plan was coming to fruition; I could see the two falling in love before my eyes.

Caspar could hardly function when she was in the room, he almost choked on his taco one night, and I thought he may actually die of embarrassment when Tessa started to perform the Heimlich on him.

I had to fight back the urge to pee from laughing so hard at the glares he sent my way the rest of that night.

We had become the best of friends. The oddest pair, with staff on the floor assuming he was the best grandson they had ever met in their careers. We often talked late into the night, looking out the window at the stars when the air became a little too cold to sit under them directly. He would tell me about his life, and I often did nothing but listen. He confided that he was feeling better these days, that he didn't think about suicide since the day he met me. He once told me I was the best therapist he had ever seen.

Truth be told, I just couldn't fathom how he had survived all that he had and still been capable of such love. I was in awe of him a lot of the time, and constantly found myself distracted while he talked, wondering if I had made my own daughter feel how he did. Misunderstood, desperate, and confused about what to do with themselves. I wished I had the chance to listen to my darling Elena confess her feelings to me, and so I listened with my whole being. I let him get it all out.

We revisited the grand piano in the lobby a lot, where he would play for me, and I would close my eyes and breathe in the music.

His footsteps halting as he came to sit at the head of my bed brought me back to the room my body was in, like a hot air balloon drifting back down to the dirt of the earth.

"Are you awake?" A hoarse voice usually meant he didn't sleep well.

I shifted in the bedsheets to look up at him.

"I just have to run home to drop off the rent cheque to my landlord."

I nodded and smiled at him. He looked as though he had aged twenty years in two weeks, and I was worried he wasn't eating enough with the way his clothes looked looser on his body.

"Come back with waffles?" I yawned, and he laughed.

"You need anything before I go?"

"Water please." I gestured towards bedside table, where my water glass with a long plastic straw sat. I felt the bed move, as Caspar pushed one of the buttons to raise my head.

He helped me to drink my water, before leaving for a little while.

I started noticing the way he would linger in the doorframe just a few days ago, staring at me even when he left to use the restroom. It was like he was cataloguing a memory in case I slipped away while he was gone.

I stuck my tongue out at him this time, wanting my memory to be one with some spunk. He returned the gesture and turned on his heels, and I could hear him have an awkward *hi, how are you?* interaction with Tessa just outside the doorway.

I had come to adore the woman for her charming personality and striking resemblance to the strong women of the feminist movement. She was confident in a way that made you always feel safe around her. She had such a calming presence.

I waved at her as she danced her way into the room.

"Hi Ansa, how are you feeling today?" She

came to my bedside and picked my hand up in her own, squeezing tightly.

"My throat feels so dry." I scrunched my nose in pain as I swallowed down saliva. "It feels like sandpaper."

"I'll let Lorraine know, it's probably one of the side effects of the new medications," she said, squeezing my hand again.

The doctors had started a more aggressive pain management regime, as my organs were failing faster than anticipated. There was some worry I wouldn't even make it to my lethal injection date.

As if reading my mind, Tessa sat beside me, looking concerned.

"What are you thinking about?" she asked.

"Just how different this pain is," I replied. She didn't ask for further explanation.

We sat in silence for a few moments before Tessa started telling me about the day's schedule. Her red hair was pulled back into that lopsided bun she liked to perch atop her head, with straggles of curly hair breezing beside her face.

Her ID badge was adorned with stickers, happy faces, and flowers. How fitting, since she was quite literally a ray of sunshine in the darkest of moments.

Caspar was a dark moment.

"Do you fancy my grandson?" I asked, matter-of-factly.

She stiffened in her chair. "Well, that's a new response to asking if we're having dinner together tonight again."

"I see the way you look at him," I said, reaching for her hand. I needed her to understand. "It's the way I looked at my husband when we started dating and the way my daughter looked at university applications."

"You've never told me about your daughter." She was changing the subject, but her eyes still showed nothing but genuine curiosity.

"It's a sad story," I said, brushing it off, "and you're such a happy woman."

"I'm sorry, Ansa."

I waved her off. "Don't be, but if you like Caspar, if you feel something in your heart—listen to it. I wish I had; I wish I had understood how courageous it is to follow your heart before it was too late. That's all."

I closed my eyes, my throat sore after talking for so long.

She stayed with me a while longer, paging Lorraine to come and increase some medications for the pain in my throat.

She squeezed my shoulder before she left, and I was thankful to have gotten to know such a kind soul. Even if I had become a crazy old lady obsessed with matchmaking on her deathbed.

Before I knew it, sleep overcame my senses.

When I woke again, it was to the sound of laughter and the smell of chicken. There were takeout containers on the hospital table in front of me and music playing from the radio Tessa brought in for our dinners from the lounge.

I peered through my eyelids, and almost squealed with excitement as I saw the two of them dancing together to the music.

Caspar spun her around, and held her in his arms, a little too close and tight to be just friends.

I smiled and closed my eyes. Not out of tiredness or pain this time, but wanting to give them this moment to themselves. Periodically I would watch them through a crack in my eyelids, peeking over the hospital blankets and willing the music to continue playing because I had never seen him smile like that before. It was the smile I recognized on my daughter's face when her father told her she could do anything in the world. It was a feeling of being infinite and somehow managing to find our way together.

It was a fleetingly small moment in time, one that came and went just as a shooting star. But it was the feeling that lingered in the room after that tiny moment, the beating of hearts in unison, the feeling of being alive, that brought a smile to my face as I heard them leave together, both squeezing my hands before heading for the garden to sit under the stars together.

I was okay with staying behind this time.

CHAPTER FIFTEEN

Tessa

The weeks since Herb passed had gone by in a blur.

I had meetings that felt like I was begging for my job, I had lost all sense of security at work—besides from the man who started to make butterflies fly in my stomach when I saw him with his grandmother, who was just as kind as he was.

It was strange, because half of my world felt like it was falling apart, yet the other half felt like a new construction zone full of optimism for what the future held.

We started having dinners together, and my dad started picking me up a few hours later than usual on a regular basis, without me having to let him know I would be late.

One night, it was pouring rain as I ran to the cab of the pickup truck.

The heat was blasting in the truck, and I leaned over to give my dad a sideways hug and kissed Charlie on his head, booping his nose with my finger and sticking my tongue out to match his.

We drove home, the heat prickling my cheeks and rain still dripping off my hair onto my shoulders.

"So," my dad said and looked at me sideways, "what's his name, Tess?"

"*What*?"

"Oh please," he laughed, "a dad knows, okay?"

I shook my head and stayed silent, petting Charlies furry head which was resting in my lap.

"Just promise me to be careful with that heart of yours, that's all."

I nodded and kissed him on the cheek, which he promptly wiped away with the sleeve of his shirt, a disgusted look on his face. He was never one for touchy-feely affection.

The next morning, Ansa asked me if I fancied her grandson, and I wondered just how easy of a book love was, that all these people around me seemed to be in on the joke before I had even realized it existed.

I went through the rest of the day feeling like a deer in the headlights.

I *knew* I fancied her grandson.

We had our new daily meeting with the budgeting team to discuss my daily tasks, responsibilities, and time commitments. It was like being a child monitored for success in school, no matter what I told them I was doing with my day, they looked at me like I was four-years-old.

I started wearing more professional clothes to work, hoping it would make me look more like an asset to the team. My bright colours were replaced with navy and grey, and I had about twenty bobby pins holding the stubborn curls that wanted to escape the neatly placed bun at the back of my head.

I felt the room go quiet as I walked in, the butterflies in my stomach feeling as though they had been caught in a rainstorm and drowned.

I gulped, feeling as though the room could notice my unease.

I couldn't remember their names, or maybe I just didn't want to.

They were all white men in power, and their inherent bias was evident from our first meeting. They had taken one look at my neon-coloured pants and scoffed at me when I tried to explain the emotional benefit of animal therapy for patients who were on our floor. I knew after the first meeting that day, which also happened to be the very next day after Herb's memorial service, that I would have to change the way I approached them if I had any hope of keeping my job.

Today, the room was tenser than normal.

"Good morning, Miss. Murphy," one of the suits said.

"Tessa, please. Good morning everyone," I replied.

"Right then, Tessa, let's get started here—what is on your calendar today?"

Lorraine sat beside me, having to come to the morning touchpoints as my clinical leader. Unfortunately, that was the depth of her role and despite her best efforts to ensure my job was saved, I knew she didn't have the power to have the final say in the matter. She patted my leg under the table, and I smiled at her before straightening my posture.

"Today we will be holding a gardening program outdoors, and I also have our pastor coming for some bedside visits. Then this evening we will be doing our exercise class before I do individual counselling sessions."

One of the suits scribbled in his notebook, underlining something, and did not look up as he said, to his colleague next to him, "Have we asked if the physio department can delegate that exercise class to an assistant of theirs?"

His colleague shook his head. "I will email the head of PT/OT this afternoon and see."

There was nothing else, and they closed their notebooks and managed to fake a smile before they both rose from the table with their coffee cups in hand.

"Wait," I said as they reached the doorway.

"The exercise class combines mental health elements too. We end with meditation moments and self-reflection, it's a lot more wholesome and in depth than a simple stretch class or anything you could just pull off the internet. It is a lot more than what it sounds like—maybe you should come and see the class yourself? Or even the garden program, I can send you a few calendars invites your way and if you can fit them into your day…" I trailed off, my voice breaking as they looked at one another.

They left, mumbling something about seeing if they could make it work or trying to make time in their busy days. I didn't recognize the look in their faces until they were gone.

It was pity.

I hoped I never had to see that look again and willed myself to get up from the chair and walk back to the unit with my chin up and my eyes forward, instead of looking at the floor like the sad puppy I felt like.

On my way back to the floor, however, I saw him, and the butterflies fluttered from somewhere at the bottom of the puddle in my stomach.

He had stopped shaving, I noticed.

I liked it. He looked real, raw, and in touch with his emotional side. He still blushed when we passed each other in the hallways, despite the shared time together these past few weeks. And the shared feelings. I wasn't sure if he was blind to the way I looked at him, or if he was just afraid to admit he felt the same way. Regardless, I ran over to him outside of Ansa's room and he stopped in his tracks. Lorraine gave me a warning glance before retreating to the nursing station.

I smiled at him. "How are you today, friendly ghost?"

Ansa had gotten the nickname to stick somehow, with half of the nursing staff calling him it, along with the other patients on the unit.

Caspar leaned against the railing in the hallway, and I moved closer to him to allow a stretcher to pass us by.

"Good, just have a couple errands to run. Ansa's tired today, she woke up with a sore throat and puked a couple times overnight."

I peered around him into the room to see Ansa curled up under the sheets. I sighed, knowing that date written in red on our whiteboard in the nurse's station was inching closer day by day; she was like a fleeting moment in time.

Everyone knew she had an expiry date, and it was a strange shift on the floor. We didn't have many patients accepted into the Medical Assistance in Dying program due to the complex requirements and legal fees. It wasn't nearly as accessible as it should be for those in pain, suffering through those final weeks and months.

"I'll go sit with her while you're out, gardening isn't for another hour."

"Thanks, Tess."

I felt blush tingling my cheeks, and the butterflies shook the water from their wings as he worked up the courage to pull me into a small hug.

If my job wasn't already almost definitely soon to be a thing of the past, I may have worried about the implications of that hug.

I wrapped my arms around him and closed my eyes for the brief few seconds and let myself feel the butterflies.

He turned and left quickly after that, and I

wondered if he had gone as red as a tomato or as a cherry.

I spun to see half the nursing team gawking and teasing, and Lorraine scowling at me. She had told me it was risky behaviour, especially while being monitored by the corporate side of the hospital and my job being on the chopping block.

Instead, I had embraced the carefree spirit that Herb would have wanted me to have and bowed to my audience before going into Ansa's room.

I stayed with her while she rested, cutting out pieces of fabric to restock our blanket weaving craft bin. We donated all the little blankets to the animal shelter, and they would send us photos of little puppies and kittens all cozied up in the fleece we had tied together. It was something that brought pure joy to everyone involved. I cut the fleece into little strips of fabric and thought about the furry babies they would soon keep warm.

Caspar returned just before I had to take my

leave for gardening.

"Will you be joining us for dinner tonight?" Caspar asked after he had settled into his chair.

"Yeah, sorry about last night. I had a crazy day and had to just go home to decompress."

I wondered when it had become so easy to tell him the truth. I felt the same way with his grand-mother as well; it was such a safe space to be your-self. Something I had always tried to ensure was that this floor was for anyone who ever wound up in our little community.

He nodded in understanding, and then Ansa sputtered a cough. He instinctively reached for the tiny trash can at her bedside and brushed her gray hair which had started to fall out these past few weeks, away from her face.

The way he cared for her left the butterflies suspended midflight.

I left then, but the scene stayed in my mind all day.

After bringing everyone back to their rooms once we had spent some time in the garden, watering the plants together and chatting, I stopped at our community photo wall and replaced the photos from last month with new ones from this month. I placed the old photos in my folder, to join the growing collection I had at home. I held the photo of Herb and me at one of our recent patio barbeques, eating burgers together with barbeque sauce smeared on his face. I tucked the photo away with a smile, thinking about where it would fit onto the growing collage on my bedroom wall at home.

The suits came around the corner just as I was taking the last photo of myself and Herb off the wall, and I fought the urge to give them a tour around the floor to boast about the positive experiences we were capturing on this wall being just a glimpse at the feeling of those small moments.

How do you put a price tag on a happy memory? Especially one made when people were essentially knocking on death's door?

They sure seemed to make it easy, as they pasted a fake smile on their faces and one of them clapped a hand on my back.

"This is a lovely photo board. Would you consider maintaining this kind of a thing on a volunteer basis?"

I scoffed and almost said something very out of character. Thankfully, they read the expression on my face, and continued to walk past the patient artwork wall, around the corner to the nursing station.

Lorraine looked surprised to see them, and I also wondered if I had missed a scheduled meeting in my calendar when I looked this morning.

"Can we chat for a few moments; we have some unfortunate news from the board."

CHAPTER SIXTEEN

Caspar

The door to the loft clicked as I turned my key in the lock. I had come home for a quick shower in a *real* shower, not one that reminded me of a college dorm locker room, and to pick up some dinner on my way back to Ansa.

My eyes caught the neon green time on the stove. I found myself constantly feeling rushed to get back to the hospital, minutes seeming like hours away from her. I was worried my phone would beep and buzz with horrible news the minute I took my sneakers off and hung my coat up.

But it didn't.

I took a long shower, by my standards, and

found a stranger looking back at me in the mirror. I hadn't let my facial hair grow this long since I was a senior in college. It was strange, and I felt like any minute my mum would burst into the room and tell me to shave my damn mug before my grandmother rolls in her grave. Thinking about my mum had started to feel good over the past while, instead of bringing urges of opening my veins to the world and letting go. The pain had resided, both in my head and in my wrist. Ansa had me on a strict regime of practicing on the grand piano in the hospital lobby when the emergency rooms were empty and the streetlights were on through the large windows. After she caught me doing physio exercises with my wrist one day she always on my case about why I don't do it more often. Every time I take out my pills she questions if I need them or if I need to play something on the piano.

At first, it really upset me. I felt judged and offended at the accusation of 'milking' my injury, but then I realized she had a point. And so I went to play the piano, and cringed when I missed notes, or when my fingers cramped.

Whenever I got frustrated and would grumble something, she would simply say to start again.

I was surprised at how healthy I looked; I no longer resembled a ghost. I pulled my long hair into a ponytail at the base of my skull, staring myself down in the fogged-up bathroom mirror. It was curious, how meeting a dying woman had somehow brought me back to life. I was eating three meals a day, I was exercising by walking to and from the hospital a few times a day, and I had someone to talk to. I was truly feeling alive, in the way I had before the accident.

Since the memorial for Herb, when Ansa told me about her grand finale she had planned, and the process and work she had put into advocating for her rights to assisted dying, I couldn't stop talking to her. It was like the one secret between us had been exposed, and all that was left was our shared secret of her not really being my grandmother. Between us there was no reason to lie or hold back, and so we spent hours just talking about anything and everything. My boss checked in now and then, seeing when I would be ready to come back to work and I never really had a solid answer. He was a good guy though, and just told me to take my time and keep in touch. I had told him a few weeks back that I had recovered from the flu but that my grandmother was now in hospital and going to leave us any day now. He understood, and I felt bad lying about our relationship when he told me he would keep my grandmother in his prayers.

So life had become trips home to the flat, yet feeling tethered to the hospital because of the peculiar bond shared between myself and Ansa.

I was back at her bedside within an hour, hair still dripping wet down my back.

She slept a lot more now than when we had first met a few weeks ago. Today was a bad one, and we spent most of the afternoon in silence. She would wake up a few times an hour either for bathroom as-sistance from the nurses, or a sip of water which I would help her with by angling the straw towards her mouth.

I decided to stay close, since she wasn't look-ing so well tonight, and ordered in some fried chick-en for dinner. The delivery driver showed up a few moments before Tessa did, radio in hand.

"How is she doing?" she asked, leaning in the doorway.

"Bad day, barely said more than two words all day." I looked at Ansa where she slept soundly.

Tessa flitted into the room and plugged the radio into the outlet next to the bed. She pressed play and soft piano music filled the room.

She had become something. I wasn't sure when, or how, or what even… All I knew was that I couldn't breathe properly when she was in the room. I knew I couldn't stop watching the way her smile tugged at her eyes, or the way she pulled her sweater sleeves over her hands when she was nervous. I noticed her, more than I had ever noticed anyone in my life. I had relationships over the years, all nice women but none that ever left me feeling this way. It was as though gravity left the room with her, and I was suspended in place until she returned.

But I didn't want to seem psychotic, so I kept those romantic spiels to myself and tried to behave like a normal human being in front of her.

Ansa was the only one I would tell, she said she had seen it written in the stars and was confident that we were meant to be more than friends. I told her I was confident she was loopy from the pain medications, and she had playfully punched my shoulder.

"Lost in thought, are we?"

"What?" I muttered, coming back to the room.

"I asked, how are you doing today?"

"Are you asking as a professional or as a friend?" I cringed at my own awkwardness.

"Friend, definitely." She laughed, and then her face shifted, "I probably won't be here 'professionally' much longer anyhow."

"What do you mean?" I asked.

"Budget cuts, corporate shenanigans." She shrugged and grabbed the takeout container closest to her and started unpacking the food.

"You can't be serious. How can they just cut a whole department?"

She laughed and looked at me like I was speaking a different language, a mixture of pity and confusion on her face.

"They don't see what I do as worthy of even being a department, Cas."

She started calling me that just last week, the first time she had it brought goosebumps to my arms. I don't know why, but I loved it. Ansa started calling me it too, but she did it to see if she could get me to blush, and to try and get a rise out of me. Often, we behaved like siblings with a rivalry.

"That's so messed up. You give people pur-pose, something to fill the days with and some laugh-ter and smiles in these hard times."

She only shrugged and smiled

"Sorry, I just—I can't imagine this place without you. I can't imagine these patients not hav-ing you here just because of budget cuts and a cor-porate world."

Another nod, another smile.

"Thank you," she whispered, avoiding my gaze. I noticed her eyes were brimming with tears, so I changed the subject.

"I got you that extra gravy, as requested last time." I slid the container of gravy towards her.

She laughed, the room less tense, and we ate and chatted about the weather and other small life things. She told me her dog ate a pair of her socks last night, the whole pair, no evidence left behind. I told her I hadn't collected my mail in so long the post office called and let me know they would be holding it all at the office until my box was emptied. We chatted about those little things for an hour or so until the subject resurfaced.

"Are you—are you going to fight for your job?"

"I have been, it's been a rough month or so, actually even longer since this first came up as something they were considering a few years ago. It just gets so tiring, especially when it feels like they aren't listening."

"I will listen, Tessa," I said and leaned back in my chair.

Ansa laid next to us, still not awake for dinner.

I watched Tessa hold her hand and trace the veins with her thumb.

"I give everything to this place, to these people, and the last thing I care about is the paycheque. I live at home still, I don't have a lot of bills—but how can they just decide that what I do is meaningless, without even giving me a chance to really show them what a difference this job makes?"

She looked at me seriously.

"It's just bullshit."

I gasped at this, and Tessa laughed.

"Apologies, I just was unaware you knew how to swear," I said, laughing.

She rolled her eyes and stuck her tongue out, and I thought my heart may explode from inside my chest.

"It is though, they come here and they make these massive decisions even though they have no idea what it entails. I wish I could just get them to shadow me for a day to see what it's like. Hold the hand of a dying person, hold the hand of a grieving widow, calm the storms that arise on a daily basis—and then instead of budget cuts it would be job postings to add to my team of one. I just think if it was someone they loved in these beds, they would make a different decision. Instead, they just come in, talk money, and leave."

She sighed and leaned back in her chair.

"I am, for lack of a better word, completely screwed."

"You know, we could try and make them see. If they only talk money, maybe you just have to speak their language," I said.

"What do you mean?" she asked, intrigued.

"I mean, we plan something to raise some money, and see if we can hit a target to ensure your role is funded in the next year's budget."

"You really think that would work?"

"Can't hurt to try, at least then we can make them see the impact."

She sat in silence for a few moments, and I worried I had overstepped out of passion and wanting to help the woman I had feelings for.

Hell, if I had the money, I would probably just write a damn cheque on the spot.

"You are a goddamn genius!" she squealed as

she jumped up from her chair.

"Holy smokes, the curse words are flying now. I guess one was all it took to break the seal, huh?" I said, laughing.

She bounced over to my chair and grabbed my hands before pulling me up to wrap her arms around me and squeeze.

She was hugging me, and I could feel the warmth of her body against mine and I thought I would melt into a puddle right there in the middle of the room. I checked to see if Ansa was awake, sure she would ridicule me for my face in this moment of hesitation, before I gently wrapped my arms around her waist.

It felt like the first rainfall after a drought.

"Thank you," she murmured against my shoulder.

She pulled away, and my arms hesitated on her waist.

"You're welcome, although I am not sure I

really did anything." I scratched at my neck and awk-wardly put my hands in my pockets to stop myself from reaching for her again.

"You gave me back my hope, you gave me an idea when I thought I had crossed them all off of my list and was ready to accept my fate without giving it my all." She shook her head, disappointed in herself.

Tessa started to pace the room, planning her next move in the corporate battle.

I sat back in my chair and held Ansa's hand in my own. I willed her to wake up and save me from embarrassing myself anymore in front of Tessa. But she stayed silent, and her eyes stayed closed.

There was a hand on my shoulder, and it made me jump.

"Sorry, I'm so sorry, I shouldn't have brought work drama into the room. I'm usually a lot more professional, I just feel safe being myself around you."

"No need to apologize."

"Should I leave you have some time alone?"

"No," I said a little too quickly, and I turned to face Tessa. "You said you were here as a friend, anyhow. Friends help friends."

She nodded and went back to pacing the room and talking about planning this event.

"I will pitch it to them tomorrow, I will see what amount they need me to raise to prove myself and we will see if they take the offer. Maybe we could do a talent show of some sort?"

I nodded and kept holding Ansa's hand in mine. I had an idea, but I wasn't sure if I should say it aloud or not. But all it took was one look at Tessa, her head down, chewing her nails and worrying about her future, before I was stumbling over my tongue to get the words out fast enough.

"I can do it; I can do a show. I am a little fa-mous in the realm of classical music, I used to com-pete nationally—I went to school for piano, it was my life's sole purpose for so long, I am rusty with this wrist but give me some time and I can do it. We can invite everyone I know who will pay top dollar, the professors and etcetera. They will pay whatever just to hear me play again, and now I am hearing myself sounding incredibly cocky so I will just shut—"

She cut my words off by pulling me out of my chair again.

"You would do that—you would do all of it—for me?" she asked.

"Yes."

"But why?"

I looked at her, an expression on her face of curiosity and intense wondering. I heard the radio again, the sweet and soft piano echoing through the room and through my heart. Maybe it was the beautiful woman in front of me, or maybe it was the idea of playing a concert in front of an actual audience of paying patrons, but I felt inspired. The kind of inspired I had only felt while seated on a piano bench, in front of an audience. The kind of inspired I never thought I would feel again, all those times I had aim-lessly swallowed pills out of sheer fear of never feel-ing this way again. The words came to my mouth, before my brain even had time to register them.

"Tessa," I said, "will you dance with me?"

CHAPTER SEVENTEEN

Tessa

He looked at me with a serious face, but with a slight smile tugging at his lips.

I could feel my heartrate pick up as I grabbed his hand and leaned in close to the warmth of him.

He held me and we spun around in delicate circles, the moment faded just as quickly as it had started. I willed the song to keep playing, as I rested my head on his chest, and breathed in the scent of rain and pine trees. My wish went unanswered, and when the song ended, we awkwardly pulled away from each other and took our seats beside Ansa in bed again. We sat in silence for a few songs before I caught him staring at me.

"Thank you," I said softly, "I can't believe you would do all that for me."

I thought I caught Ansa peeking at us underneath her sunken eyelids, but I shook my head and looked back at Caspar, who was smiling at me.

His hair was dishevelled, a few strands fallen from the perfect ponytail at the nape of his neck.

"Ansa likes to look at the stars."

"Your grandmother and you have such an amazing relationship." I smiled at the small woman, and the way he held her hand in his own.

"Yeah," he mumbled quietly, "she's been there for me when I needed her most."

I could see tears forming in his eyes and squeezed her hand in mine. All three of our spirits were connected in that moment.

"She would want us to go and get a closer look, I think." He gestured to the stars outside the window. We both squeezed her paper-thin hands and then as we left the room, I felt his fingers brush against my hand. In the most natural movement, he delicately folded my hand into his.

We walked out of the room hand in hand, Lorraine's eyebrows shooting off her face from behind the nursing station as we jogged our way to the red exit sign at the end of the hallway. The metal doors burst open; it was pouring rain. I skidded to a stop, but he kept going, pulling me by my hand into the puddles of the community garden lawn, the cold drops of rain splattering us as they fell from the sky.

He looked up, hand still holding mine, and closed his eyes.

I could see the few patients on the floor who were still awake, coming to their windows and watching us along with the nursing staff and a flustered Lorraine.

I looked at them and contemplated taking a safer route, returning inside and ending the show right then and there. We must have looked insane. But when I squinted through the rain, and saw the smile stretched on the always cynical face of Marge, I wondered why anyone would ever fight this feeling in their chest—the one of being utterly and completely alive. Not just living, not just breathing, but being alive in every sense of the word.

My eyes settled on the small wooden cross in the garden, surrounded by the flowers we had planted a few weeks ago for Herb.

And suddenly, I could hear him in the back of my skull.

'Promise me, that you will keep true to who your heart tells you to be. Ignore everything else, that's where I went wrong.'

I would listen, I told myself, as I closed my eyes and tipped my head up, letting the rain hit my face.

'Nothing else matters when you are here, not a damned thing can come with you. So just, just listen to what your heart wants at all costs.'

I squeezed Caspar's hand in my own.

'Here I go.'

Me too, Herb, me too.

I whirled around and put my hands on his shoulders.

"Has anyone told you that you are incredibly handsome?"

"What?" He laughed and blushed, surprised.

"I mean it," I said, taking hold of his hands. "You are incredible, and you make me feel like I am breathing again for the first time in years, like I am really being myself when I am around you. I don't know everything about you, but I know enough to know I want to know more, if that makes sense?"

"Should we go inside? Are you feeling okay?" He laughed and tried to drop my hand, like he couldn't believe what I was saying, but I held on tighter.

"Why don't we go outside in the rain more often? Why do you think we stop jumping in puddles when we grow older? And why do we stop making mud pies and collecting rocks?"

Caspar looked at me like I was a crazy person for a moment, but then his eyes lit up.

"She isn't my grandma. I met her a month ago in the Emergency department."

I laughed, and his eyebrows shot up.

"Laughter was not the reaction I was expecting!" he shouted over the increasing rainfall, smiling big.

"I think I'm falling for you, despite the foundation of lies that is now our relationship!" I shouted back.

"Our relationship?" he sputtered.

I stretched towards him on my tiptoes, aware of the audience we still had watching us from inside the building.

And I kissed him.

CHAPTER EIGHTEEN

Caspar

It was like fire meeting ice.

I was happy to melt.

CHAPTER NINETEEN

Tessa

When our lips parted, he laughed in disbelief and squeezed my hand.

"Wow."

"*Wow* is right." I squeezed his hand back,

"Seriously though, you're going to get sick being out in this weather, let's get dried off." He turned around and noticed all the eyes watching us from the building.

"You know, that's a myth. The rain making you sick thing?" I laughed again and looked at the way the stars seemed to be crying down on us. Tears of joy, not sadness.

He shook his head at me, and whispered, "I

think I may have gotten you in some trouble, we have an audience."

"I bet they would all like to jump in the puddles again. I wish I could bottle up this feeling and share it with them when we go back inside."

He wrapped an arm around my shoulders, and I let him lead us back inside. Lorraine opened the door and handed us both towels, having had shooed the rest of the staff away from the windows. She shook her head at me as we dried off, two wet dogs drying off at the back door.

"I hope to hell you are putting your nametag back on and clocking back in to help me settle all these patients back in bed from the little soap opera the two of you decided to put on this evening."

I thought she was genuinely mad at me for a fleeting moment, until she cracked a grin and patted Caspar on the shoulder.

"Good luck keeping her out of trouble, Lord knows I have been trying for years, and look what kind of response I get."

She turned and mumbled something about kids being kids under her breath, before winking at me over her shoulder and giving me a thumbs up.

I rolled my eyes at my friend, before noticing the weight of Caspar's eyes on me.

"You're soaked."

"I have extra clothes in my locker. I'll change and meet you back in Ansa's room."

And then I remembered the truth he had shared with me, during our rainy escape. They were not related; they were strangers who crossed paths in an emergency department. I had a million questions, and Caspar must have noticed, because he lowered his face to mine and pressed his lips gently to my forehead.

"Later," he said against my forehead.

He was walking back to Ansa's room before I had time to say anything more. I felt heat prickle the spot he had kissed on my forehead.

When I got to my locker, there were four nurses on their dinner breaks, who were instantly out of their chairs asking me questions. I dodged most of them with simple answers.

"Aren't you afraid of getting in trouble?" one of them asked, but Lorraine came in at just the right moment to save me from answering that difficult question.

There was a part of me that almost told everyone his secret, about not being related to her, and how there were no issues with us having a relationship, before I realized that wasn't my secret to share.

"She won't get in trouble because everyone will keep their mouths shut until they kiss again once his grandmother is no longer her patient—correct, Tessa?"

"Correct, boss lady," I said, as I opened my locker and grabbed a fresh pair of trackpants, and the green sweatshirt Herb had given me. Lorraine looked at the sweater and sighed. She knew how I felt about getting to know our patients, she knew they were always family to me. Despite the grief, the pain, the loss, it was just how I was.

I changed in the washroom, and when I came back out it was just Lorraine sitting at the table in the middle of the locker room.

"Promise me something?" she asked, leaning back in her chair.

"Anything, Lorraine."

"Next time you decide to wake up the entire floor ten minutes before my shift ends, and distract the entire staff from giving reports on time, can you make sure I'm on vacation?"

I thought I would choke on the laughter, as I collapsed into the chair across from her.

"Am I losing my mind?"

"That's what love does, my friend. The important thing is that you have people like me to cover for your crazy ass when you decide to lose your mind at the wrong time in the wrong place."

"Thank you, Lorraine," I said. She just nodded and clicked her tongue at me again before getting up and putting a hand on my shoulder.

"He's damn cute."

"Isn't he?" I asked, excitedly.

"No, that was a test. Wrong place, wrong time."

"Sorry, uh," I laughed, "—who are you talking about?" She rolled her eyes.

"Better, now go spend time with Ansa. Not her grandson."

I contemplated sharing his secret again, relieving Lorraine of some of the stress I had just created for her, but I stopped myself and instead gave her a quick hug and hurried out of the room.

Ansa was still asleep, and Caspar was again holding her hand in his own, only he was in dry clothes now. He smiled at me, as I leaned in the doorframe.

"Come and sit with us?" he asked. I apologized to my dad in my head at the fact he would have to come pick me up late again. He was starting to get used to my late-night pick-up requests though, and he didn't seem to mind, or if he did, he didn't let on between the questions about this boy he assumed I liked.

I smiled at the man I would introduce to him and wondered why I felt so sure about it.

I walked into the room and pulled the plastic chair that was opposite him, over to the same side of the bed as him. I sat down, and an awkward air filled the room.

"So…" I started.

"I should have told you a while ago, I wanted to tell you a while ago," he explained.

"Are there any more secrets?" I asked.

He smiled, but there was a sad silence to the way it sat on his face.

"She saved me from myself."

I reached for his hand, and his fingers closed

around mine. We were again connected, all three. I knew there was so much more to talk about, a million questions raced through my mind, but for now I was content with just enjoying the moment.

"Are you ready for something like this?" I asked, unsure how to word the question.

"I want to try," he said, swallowing.

"Me too," I said.

The awkward tension left the room, and I leaned my head on his shoulder. He had turned the small radio back on; the music seemed to echo the sound of his heartbeat. I don't know how, but we spent two hours like that. In complete silence, somehow getting to know one another better.

He took moments to trace the lines on my hand with his thumb, and I tried to memorize the way his shoulder perfectly fit my head. The way he stilled when I moved, trying to make sure he was keeping me comfortable. I shivered at one point, only slightly, but he noticed and quickly took off his sweater and wrapped it around my shoulders.

"I told you would get sick out there."

"And I told you," I said and rested my chin on his shoulder, looking into his eyes, "that is a big fat lie."

I stuck my tongue out at him, and he brushed a curly tendril of hair out of my face, before kissing me gently.

"You should get some rest, that cafeteria coffee only goes so far," he whispered against my head.

I found myself starting to get dizzy from tiredness as I noticed the time on my phone, and quickly texted my dad to come and pick me up.

"You're right," I mumbled.

"Don't go feeding that ego of his, girl," a small voice coughed from the bed. We both jumped a bit at the sound of her voice, and she wheezed with laughter.

"Nice to see the two of you finally came to your damn senses."

"We've only known each other for a month," Caspar responded.

"Don't ever treat time like it is anything but fleeting my friends, make every second count."

I felt my phone vibrate in my pocket, and Caspar nodded at me.

"I'll walk you out," he said.

I thought I would have a heart attack from happiness when he tucked his hand into mine and smiled at me.

Ansa only waved, Caspar patting her on the shoulder and telling her he would be right back.

When we got to the door, I noticed Caspar holding an umbrella in his other hand. He offered it to me as the rain continued to pour down. I could see the headlights of my dad's pickup truck outside. I shook my head.

"No thanks, I think I like running in the rain."

He opened the door with a grin on his face. "See you tomorrow?"

I looked at the pickup truck and reached up to take his face in mine. I pulled him towards me and kissed him lightly. Then I opened the door and stuck my hand out into the weather.

The rain felt warmer, or maybe it was just me.

Either way, I grinned and ran through the raindrops, pausing to jump into a puddle before swinging open the door to the pickup truck and climbing in.

"That must be him," my dad said by way of a greeting. I just kept grinning; I couldn't stop.

"Is he nice to you?"

"Of course he is," I said.

"Good." He pulled me into a sideways hug and kissed the top of my head.

We were almost home, and I was half asleep in the passenger seat, when I heard him whisper, under his breath.

"You'll always be my little girl."

CHAPTER TWENTY

Ansa

I watched them fall in love, day by day, moment by moment. I also started to wonder if I would make it to my own grand finale.

It became a chore to stay awake, my body wanted to protect itself from the pain by sleeping it off and hoping we would feel better after a fourteen-hour nap. We never did though, and it was like my brain was frantically searching for a solution when there were no options left. Breathing started to feel like it took every muscle in my body, instead of just something that happened without any thought. I hated myself for taking those simple things for granted. I spent more time crying, more time wishing I had more time. I didn't think I would have these days, I thought that choosing Medical Assistance in Dying would eliminate all the other parts of the dying process, but I had been wrong. I still felt the reaper inching closer, and I still feared the absolute nothingness that awaited me. I had days where I doubted any religion, and I had days where I wanted to be baptised into all of them at once.

Caspar was there through it all.

He became the stronger of us, our roles reversed.

Tessa became a permanent fixture in our story as well, and I found myself bearing witness to the beginning of something wonderful. Sometimes I woke from sleep to hear them confessing things to each other, hear them getting to know one another in the same way my husband and I had early on in our relationship.

I would smile and pretend to sleep a while longer, enjoying the memories of my own youth and my own conversations and professions of love with my family.

I willed them to fight for that, to fight for what felt right.

A few weeks went by like this. We were planning a benefit show to raise funds for the hospital, indirectly funding Tessa's role that the big boys in their suits promised she could keep—if we could raise the proposed funding.

She told us that they had laughed at the idea, that they had shot it out of the air but agreed with expressions of pity on their faces. It pained me to watch the way she shrunk in on herself when she mentioned it.

My heart filled when I heard Caspar tell her we would prove them wrong. He was everything I knew he was, from that moment he returned my pink glasses and talked with me.

I sat in bed, the ache in my spine tingling as they had just repositioned me, so I could eat.

I scooped some pea puree onto my spoon, my nose scrunching in disgust.

Tessa laughed from where she sat on the blanket on the floor. It was her day off, but she was still here.

"If you think it's funny, let's see you try some baby food." I offered the spoonful in her direction.

She put her hands up. "No thank you, but you know we can't sneak you any more snacks that you may choke on." She shot a pointed look at Caspar, "Right, Caspar?"

"I made him do it, cut him some slack," I said in defense.

"How can you deny a dying woman ice cream, do you even have a heart, Tess?"

She feigned horror before she stuck her tongue out at him. The sunlight warmed my feet under the blanket as I watched them.

"So where are we on the project?" I nodded towards the papers strewn about the floor where they sat.

Caspar scratched at his neck and leaned back on his elbows. "Just about ready to send out invitations."

The past weeks we had spent all free time planning the big event. Tessa wanted it to be here, amongst her family members and with her patients front row. She was a lovely person, really. A heart of pure gold, and a mind of wonders. She always put people at ease, even on my worst days where it was hard to hide the pain in my expressions, she would bring a calmness into the room that would help me drift into sleep and escape the pain.

Caspar and I spent a good portion of the days together—when she was running her activities on the floor and spending time with my neighbors—talking about what a marvel she was.

"Do you have anyone you'd want to invite?" Caspar asked me.

"I have everyone I need," I smiled at the couple in front of me and scooped up more of my so-called lunch.

I meant it; I had the spirit of my husband and daughter with me and I had these two oddballs who flew in at the last minute.

"Tessa, short for Theresa?" I asked.

She hopped up and came to sit beside me.

"Just Tessa on my birth certificate, but my dad says it does come from Theresa."

"I thought so," I said, swallowing another bite of peas, "It's derived from the Greek verb meaning to harvest."

"I can't say I've ever been much for plants, despite the small garden outside."

"Well," I said, smiling, "maybe you cultivate something else. Happiness, peace, calmness, empathy, empowerment. Never forget what your impact is in this world and stick it to these suits. This place, us people, we need people like you. We need some harvesters of humanity in this world."

She smiled and took my hand in hers, staying like that while we carried on with our planning, and I hoped she would remember me. I hoped they both would.

I wondered if they would share the story of how they met at their wedding, wondered if their children would speak my name to their friends and significant others, wondered if I would live on in the memories of people on this Earth.

It was a lot to be thinking about while eating mushed up peas.

CHAPTER TWENTY-ONE

Caspar

In the span of a few weeks, a lot had happened.

Tessa and I were the talk of the hospital supposedly, but not in the bad way as we had both anticipated. It turned out it was not that big of a deal after all, and the hospital administration seemed more intent on ending Tessa's contract of employment that they didn't even blink an eye when she decided to inform them of our involvement. The benefit show now had a date, just a month away in the beginning of August– which always reminded me of the other upcoming date in our calendars.

Ansa was scheduled to die on August the 15th, and it was her birthday as well—something she found poetic, but I found disturbing, which in turn her and Tessa both found funny and worthy of mockery.

That was the other shift; we had become a trio of sorts.

And for some reason, I was always the victim of them ganging up on me. There was no exception to that rule, as we sat on the floor on our blanket at the foot of Ansa's bed, the new normal for the three of us on Tessa's lunch breaks.

"The invites should seem classy, like a piano recital programme would usually be."

I waved my drafted invitation so that both women staring at me could see.

They exchanged a glance and nodded, before saying, in unison, "No."

I shook my head and suppressed what felt like laughter and a sigh, combined. "I suppose you two have already figured it out then?"

"We were thinking more along the lines of this..." Tessa slid a notebook across the floor we were occupying, and Ansa snorted in laughter from where she sat upright in bed.

"This." I looked at the bright colours of a rainbow on the page and sighed. "This is a children's birthday party invitation, not something I can knowingly mail to all the people who legitimately taught me how to play classical music pieces."

"Yeah, well, first off—get over yourself," Ansa said and adjusted her glasses. I could see her wince in pain with movement.

Tessa covered her smile with her hand.

"Secondly—you have no say, because *I* am dying, and I like the one with the rainbow."

Tessa burst into laughter, and I slid her notebook back to her.

"Fine, but if Barney shows up, I am walking off the stage. Or will we also be moving the piano to the garden?"

They exchanged another look, one of pure excitement.

"No. Absolutely not. Think about the acoustics!" I begged.

"Think about the warmth though!" Ansa pleaded through a cracked voice.

"And the sunlight!" Tessa echoed.

I sighed and laid down on the blanket, staring up at the ceiling and wondering why I had agreed to this plan, and then instantly remembering how the two women made me feel.

I smiled at the ceiling.

"We will have to get the piano tuned again after we move it, and there has to be a tent then in case of weather."

I heard them clap their hands together.

They chatted about flowers and different ways to decorate people's chairs, I heard the words simple and classy, and then found myself lost in thought again.

I must have fallen asleep, because when I woke up the sunlight had turned into a flash of orange on the cream-coloured walls. I groaned as I sat up, my spine aching so much that I wondered why we had decided to lay on the floor in the first place.

There was a piece of paper on my chest, and I crumpled it a bit when I reached for it, before smoothing it and reading a message scrawled in curvy lettering I recognized as Tessa's. It was a script that felt comforting, just like everything else about her. It read; *you look cute asleep. see you after work.*

I stretched out and stood up to see Ansa asleep. I stretched my arms out and yawned, before placing the note from Tessa on the window ledge and walking around the room a bit. I looked at the clock on the wall and realized I only had an hour or so until Tessa was finished work. I hadn't showered or any-thing today, so I decided to take my things into the washroom and let the water run over my body.

I never left the hospital anymore, even for takeout or showers. The loft wouldn't mind sitting empty, and I didn't want to miss a moment of time with the woman in the pink glasses.

I wrapped a towel around my waist, stepped out of the shower and looked in the mirror. I was surprised at the healthy man who stared back at me, I had gained some weight and I looked brighter. My eyes were no longer brimmed in black, and I could flex each one of my fingers without wincing.

I found myself healing in more ways than one.

I often wondered when I no longer needed the pills for the physical pain, and when I started using them to self-medicate.

Nowadays, I listened to the voice in my head that told me it was okay to be afraid, it was okay to be sad, it was okay to have these feelings; I didn't have to run from them anymore, because I had time to say goodbye.

I had time, which I think was all I ever wanted with my mother. I wanted the chance to tell her that I loved her just one more time, I wanted to know

I could play the piano again and not feel broken inside.

I had found that here, with the woman in the pink glasses, with Ansa.

And with Tessa, I had found hope for the future.

I dried my hair with a towel and dressed myself. I saw the pill bottle in the bottom of my backpack, still full from when I had packed it in there a few weeks ago. The refill prescriptions must have had a layer of dust on them now, from where they sat on my kitchen counter.

I opened the door to the bathroom and saw Tessa sitting next to Ansa, who was awake and staring at me.

"You shower longer than my daughter and I ever did."

Tessa laughed. "To be fair, those showers don't always have the best water pressure."

"Tough crowd, as always," I mumbled as I

tossed my backpack onto the floor and went over to kiss Tessa on the forehead.

How she managed to still smell of vanilla after a twelve-hour shift in a hospital mystified me.

Tessa stood to give me a hug before retreating to her chair to finish the game of cards her and Ansa were playing on the foot of the hospital bed.

I pulled a chair closer to where she was, holding onto the back of it.

"I feel like I need to see a chiropractor after napping on the floor all day, but I'm thinking cafeteria coffee is a good second option. Can I get you ladies anything?"

"The usual," Ansa said with a smile. Earl grey tea with the bag still in, two sugars, and a milk on the side.

"I'm okay, thanks, one of the girls brought homemade butter tarts today, so I am all sugared up. Hungry though, can we order food when you get back?"

"Sounds like a plan, be back in a few."

I always noticed how different the regular hospital hallways were from the palliative care floor Ansa and myself had called home for the last little while.

It was like walking through a portal when the metal double doors swung open and the soft yellow walls turned to a stark pale white. Instead of lavender aromatherapy, it smelled of chemicals. Instead of hearing soft piano music playing over the radio, it was call bells beeping and codes being called. I supposed that one was because there were no codes to be called; it was the final stop for everyone. Tessa was the one who made that energy though, and I shuddered at the thought of people dying surrounded by these smells and plain colours versus the enriched endings they had with her as a friend.

I was worried we would not have enough of an impact though, I was worried that even after the concert, even if we did raise the money that she would just be put through this again as soon as they had the chance. I think she thought that too, as I often found her mind drifting away when we talked about the future.

I walked into the cafeteria, which was mostly empty aside from a janitor mopping the floors and a few patients sitting across the table from loved ones and eating stale pastries and drinking watered down coffee. It had become my favourite watered down coffee though, because of the company which I usually drank it with.

I poured my coffee first, and then placed a teabag in a cup and poured some boiling water in it. I took a third cup and filled it with the sugars and creamers required, humming under my breath. I was dabbing the tea bag into the cup and watching the colour of the tea swirl with the hot water in the cup, when I heard my name being shouted down the hallway.

As soon as I saw Tessa, I knew something

was wrong. I looked away from the swirling tea bag, to see a look of fear on her face and her eyes were wide as she found me.

She ran over, her red curls bouncing on her shoulders.

She grabbed my wrist, the bad one, and I winced.

"Caspar, come on, it's Ansa."

I was frozen in spot though; the cup was starting to burn my hand as the boiling water continued to swirl. I didn't have time to think, before my hand dropped the cup and the burning liquid spilled all over my shoes and my socks.

I looked into her eyes, as she tugged on my wrist, on the sleeve of my hoodie.

"We have to go now. Come on. I'm here with you."

Her calming voice didn't match the expression on her face, but it was enough to move me from the spot that I felt was glued to the floor.

We ran down the hallways, her leading the way with her hand grasped with mine. The light above the doorframe was on, flashing red and white.

We stood there, and I watched in horror as Lorraine was yelling at me.

I couldn't hear the words though; all I saw was the woman who laid flat on her back as another nurse pushed on her chest and kept looking between her and the monitors.

It was Tessa's voice that broke through all the noise. "Caspar, they need to know."

"What does your grandmother want done?" Lorraine yelled again.

"I... I don't know," I mumbled, not completely sure if this was actually happening or if I was still napping on the floor.

"Well, what did she tell you she wanted done? We don't have a DNR because she is scheduled for medical assistance in dying, but we also don't have express consent for CPR." I noticed now that Lorraine was also on the phone as she yelled at me.

"I've only known her for a couple months!" I shouted, tears running down my face.

"You are next of kin, aren't you?" she asked.

I shook my head no, and Lorraine muttered a curse word and told the nurse to keep doing compressions. She left the room throwing a wary glance at me and Tessa as she brushed past us. We stood there for the next hour, as they inserted a tube down her throat and monitors were ushered into the room and connected to different parts of her small body. By the time they were finished, there was a steady beeping noise in the room and there was hardly any of Ansa left. It was all monitors and wires and straps to hold things in place.

I felt exhausted suddenly, just before my knees buckled underneath me.

I fell to the floor, but Tessa was quick to bring a chair over to the hallway outside of the room. Followed by a warm blanket around my shoulders, and finally a cup of water with a bendable straw in it.

"Drink," she said.

I listened and looked at her where she bent in front of me, watching me with a careful eye.

"I am going to go explain to Lorr–"

"Please don't go," I said, desperately, reaching for her.

She squeezed my hand.

"Hey, you have to be strong now, okay? She would want that. And I am going to go stop Lorraine from doing something stupid, that would take you away from Ansa's bedside, even though we all know family can be chosen."

I swallowed heavily, my eyes welling up

"Come back soon." It was all I could manage, but she squeezed my hand again as if she understood.

And I trusted that, I trusted she would come back. Which was not always something that came easily, or without time.

She did come back, and when she did, Lorraine was with her.

I was unsure how long they had talked things over, but I was glad to see that Lorraine's face had softened, and she just looked tired now, not upset anymore.

"I'm sorry," I blurted out. "It just happened. We met each other and then it was a secret, and we became friends, and then, this, this wasn't supposed to be how things happened."

"Oh, boy." Lorraine came over and placed a reassuring hand on my back. "Life never goes the way it's planned—what matters is that you can course correct. I'm sorry if I was hard on you, Tessa explained how the two of you met. I don't appreciate being lied too, but all I care about is giving my patients good care. Just don't go telling everyone you aren't related because we don't need them kicking you out of here when Ansa would want you with her. The three of us know, let's keep it that way, okay?"

"Thank you," I said gratefully.

"She's in a coma, we don't know what happened yet," she said.

"What will happen now?" I asked.

"Well, we have to wait for her to wake up—she won't be eligible for medical assistance in dying if she is unconscious. So we keep her comfortable, and we hope she wakes up so she can go the way she had wanted to all along."

Tessa and Lorraine talked a while longer, but I didn't listen. I stared at Ansa covered in machines and wires in the room.

I stood up and walked into the room, despite my heart beating dangerously fast. I could pass out at any moment, but I needed to be in there. I never did like blood, or needles, or anything like that. But here I was, conquering my fear as I sat next to her body that seemed so void of her.

I took her hand in mine and closed my eyes, hoping I would wake up and be back on the floor before a warm shower.

CHAPTER TWENTY-TWO

Ansa

Caspar never left the room; I knew that for a fact because I was aware of his presence in the way a mother knows when something is wrong with their child.

Tessa was the one who would come and go, but he was always there. I could hear him talking to me the whole time, registering even the whispered words he spoke. I was unsure if the words I was speaking were out loud or were in my head. I willed my mouth to open and to speak, but it never felt like they came, and it took so much energy. I heard him tell me how much he loved me, and how much he wished I could hear him. I wanted to tell him I knew, I wanted to squeeze his hand back when I felt him squeeze mine.

But all I felt was an abyss of nothingness and a complete loss of control. I heard him tell me that I saved his life and I wanted to set the record straight: I wanted to scream that he had saved himself, that *he* was all he needed. All he needed was permission to love himself again, and to credit me with that—well, that just seemed tragic. But then I heard him tell me that he would be alright, that everything would be alright, that I could rest.

And so I did.

CHAPTER TWENTY-THREE

Tessa

As I stared at Ansa, I would think about the younger version of myself. I wondered if my parents had cried the way Caspar did, I wondered if I looked the same way Ansa did. So beautifully peaceful, underneath the wires and bandages.

I stayed the night, thankful that I had some vacation time to use before the imminent doom of my career. I asked Lorraine if I could take that time and she said she would be upset with me if I gave the suits any more of my time, considering the way they had been lately; taking things off the walls we had painted, talking about removing the garden outside for extra parking. Work had become more of a public show of power over me, my role, and this concert we had planned, and it just was not worth it.

So I started saying my goodbyes and resolved that I would find a way to still do what I love to do. I would find a way, I had to. But now I was taking the time earlier than anticipated. But one look at the man I had come to know, and love, made me reconsider giving up the fight. He saw me for the slightly cracked, *heads a marley*, type of Irish lass my dad raised me to be, and still found a way to love me.

I still didn't know when or how or why it had clicked, but it was like we had gone from strangers to soulmates. I felt like he knew me better than I knew myself, and I was so glad for the woman in the bed who had brought us together at a time when we needed each other most.

I watched Lorraine push a cot into the room, followed by a second one to match. Caspar was asleep, head resting in my lap, his hair just brushing my socks.

Lorraine purposefully placed the cot on opposite sides of the room, and then wagged a finger at me, just like my parents would have done when I put seven chocolate bars in the shopping cart.

I stuck my tongue out but smiled in appreciation. She really was a blessing in my life—in everyone's life—and my next mission would be to get her some more appreciation around the hospital for all the double shifts she worked, for all the money she spent on supplies for the patients that didn't have families with the means, and countless other things.

It was the end of her shift; I knew because the time on the clock confirmed Ansa had made it through the night. Lorraine checked a few of the monitors before leaving the room with a wave.

I brushed Caspar's hair from his face, he had to get up because I had to pee desperately. His eyes slowly opened, and I watched him process all the emotions just a few hours ago. I wanted to make it better, but I knew it wasn't something a bandage would fix.

"Good morning, sunshine," I mumbled and brushed another strand of hair from his face. He looked up at me, head still in my lap, and squinted through sleepy eyes.

He smiled, it was small, but it was enough to make my heart leap.

"Morning." He got up slowly and stretched his arms out in front of him with a grunt.

"Did anything change?" he asked.

I shook my head. He frowned, then looked at the cots placed ten feet apart.

"If I smell that poorly, you should have said so a while ago."

"Lorraine did that," I explained, a blush rising to my cheeks.

He laughed softly, patting me on the shoulder. The laughter left his face when he looked at Ansa, but a calm, small smile appeared instead. He smoothed the blanket near her hand, touching it briefly.

"She would want us to get those invites mailed out today. She would want us to stay busy while we wait for her to wake up."

The healthcare worker in me knew better than that, knew better than to think that she would wake up again, especially at her age and her diagnoses. I knew the next little while wouldn't be full of the peace we presently had around us. Instead, there would be multiple codes and cracked ribs until she was ripped away harshly, not in a peaceful sleep she had worked so hard to ensure she got.

More than anything, it broke my heart that she was unlikely to have her final goodbye on her own terms. It didn't seem fair of the universe to come between someone getting their final wishes honoured.

I would do my best to ignore the professional part of me though, because I couldn't be that person. I was the family, I was the friend, I was the—currently unlabelled—romantic partner. I was on the other side of the mirror now.

I looked at the glimmer of hope in Caspar's eyes and squeezed his hand.

"I think you are absolutely right." I paused, then said through a smile, "but you should consider showering if you expect me to move those cots any closer this evening."

The way we could be so casual, so familiar with each other felt like we had already been here before, maybe sometime in another life.

It was like my heart found a missing piece.

I was happy to be on the other side of the mirror for once.

I went home a little bit later in the morning to get some things and told my parents everything.

My mom, who always felt so deeply, teared up with horror and sadness as I told them about Ansa and poor Caspar. She didn't even know them but felt a deep sadness about their misfortune; I knew I had gotten that from her and was glad of it.

When my dad drove me back, duffel bag in hand, he was much more quiet than usual.

"You know, Tess," he said as we pulled into the parking lot, "you deserve to work somewhere where you are appreciated. Promise me you won't put up with that kind of narcissism even if it is what you love to do—promise me you'll find a different way, because I have to know that you are appreciated."

I nodded my agreement and went to open the door, but he stopped me with a hand on my shoulder.

"We almost lost you," he said. "Death came so close, but the universe decided you weren't finished, and I will be damned if anyone takes advantage of that caring personality of yours. You can move mountains, do you understand?"

"I promise that I've got a plan, don't worry," I said, full of love and appreciation of my father. "Love you, dad."

He gave me a big hug, and I wondered if he

always thought it would be the last time he did. I wondered if my parents lived through life with the worry of losing me at any second, since they had come so close before.

There was no time to spare that afternoon. We handmade over 500 invitations, each one personalized. I made sure Caspar took breaks, made sure he still was aware of his surroundings, made sure he was still processing the situation as much as it hurt.

I almost forgot I was at my workplace, and as I filled out invitations, I realized that the entire time I was at home, I was counting down the minutes until I was back with Caspar. I wasn't sure why I felt at home when I was with him, but I did.

It was strange, but somewhere between hello and here, there was love.

CHAPTER TWENTY-FOUR

Ansa

They were so happy because the show sold out, I could hear them celebrating and they made sure to include me. It was strange, the way they talked to one another was like they knew each other differently than when I had last been awake. I wondered how long it had been since I was properly in their company. I tried to force my eyes open just to see their faces again.

Hadn't they just started making invitations yesterday? I remember them bickering over the design of the invitation, me fueling the argument as always. Was time fleeting? Was I sleeping away the few minutes I had left of my Earthside journey? I was so upset with myself, upset with the loss of my abilities, upset with the cards that were placed in my hand. It felt like years had passed between the day they were sitting on the blanket at the foot of my bed, the day I had told Tessa the meaning of her name, and now. They both took turns hugging me, telling me the good news of the sold-out show. I willed a smile to come to my face, but the muscles felt concrete. I wondered for a second if I had actually shouted out loud in pain, or if the sounds were just echoing through my skull.

I was so unbearably tired.

CHAPTER TWENTY-FIVE

Caspar

We did it, we raised the money before the show even happened. People started buying tickets, and then more people, and then some more, and before we knew it there was nothing else to do but sit and wait for the day of the show.

Without distraction, though, I found a darkness creeping into my head. I started to stare at the bottle of pills in my backpack just a while longer, started contemplating if I was bad news for Tessa, started to feel an ache in my wrist because I had stopped doing the exercises Ansa had forced me to do.

I felt ridiculous for thinking, even for a moment, that this part of me had packed its bags and left for good.

The world just felt so unfair.

Though I was not sure she could hear me, I begged her to wake up.

I still had things I wanted to tell Ansa. And things I wished I got to say to my mother as well— it was like living through a repeat episode and not being able to understand why. My chest hurt in the same way it had months ago, and it made me want to return to my old ways. It was just easier to numb the feelings than to actually go through them. I knew how weak that sounded, but it was the truth.

But then Tessa would come into the room and wrap me in a hug or reach for my hand, and I felt guilty for even bringing her into this, into the mess-iness of me. I felt bad, and almost without realizing I started to put up a wall—I didn't talk to her about my feelings. I knew she could sense it when I would go limp in her arms or when I would withdraw from her touch. I knew she deserved better; I was lucky to have found her and I did not want to lose her, but this was my reality.

I was stuck to the chair beside Ansa's bed. The world continued to spin around us, but we remained in silence.

"I had a meeting with them this morning, did I tell you?" Tessa asked. Her hand was on my knee.

"No, I don't think so." I couldn't look at her, I was ashamed of myself.

"They were shocked when I told them the show sold out," she said.

"I bet," I said.

She stood up and started to pace.

"They asked when I can start again, because families have been complaining and moving their loved ones out," she said, matter-of-factly. "I told them I have to think about it, but…" I looked up at her when she stopped speaking and saw she was staring at me. She sat back in the chair next to me and put her hand on my knee again.

"Caspar, are you okay?"

I shook my head, unable to say anything without feeling the weight of the pill bottle I had placed in my pocket after the shower I had this morning. I was not okay, but I didn't want to drag her with me. I willed myself to be hopeful, for her.

"I'm alright, just tired and worried."

"I don't believe you," she said instantly. I laughed, not with joy, but with slightly irritation.

"You don't even know me well enough, but I don't blame you for not believing me."

I said it without thinking, and I instantly regretted it. I felt like I was being torn apart on the inside. There was the old me who was wanting to disappear, and the new me who was falling in love with this woman. They were at odds and I was stuck in the middle.

She didn't even flinch though, instead she just got up and walked to the doorway.

"Wait, Tess, I'm sorry—" She shook her head.

"No, I am sorry," she said over my stumbling words. She had her hands up and a beautiful, sad smile on her face. "There are bigger things on your mind, not some silly show or even sillier girl. I'm sorry, I'll give you some time alone. I'll be back later."

There was a part of me that wanted to get on my knees and beg her to stay; I wanted to shout out that I didn't care how long we had known each other, because I knew her on a higher level than I had known anyone else. I was connected to her from the moment I saw her, in the way the movies talked about love at first sight. She came at the exact time I needed her most, and I wanted her to know that. But the pain in my chest was too strong, and when I opened my mouth, all I could mumble was a goodbye.

I sighed and leaned back in the chair.

Fuck it.

I reached into my pocket for the pill bottle and tried to unscrew the lid, but the child proof seal was being stubborn, and my elbow knocked something off the bedside table. It was so damned cramped in this room, it felt like it was ten times smaller with all these machines and monitors cramming around the bed.

I reached underneath the bed and realized what I knocked over. It was a pair of thick glasses set in bright pink frames. I held the glasses in my hand and stared at them for a few minutes. It was a moment frozen in time, where there was nothing else in the room except for me, Ansa, and the pink glasses I held. The pill bottle in my other hand seemed to start to burn, and I ran for the bathroom.

I finally got through the child proof seal and emptied the small round tablets down the drain.

For good measure, I turned the tap on and watched the water flow down the drain. I threw the empty bottle into the trash bin and set the pink frames on the counter before falling to the floor and sobbing.

It was the kind of sobbing that physically hurt.

I wouldn't be that person again; I *couldn't* be that person again. I had to try, and if not for me, for my mother and for Tessa and for Ansa.

I wanted to live.

I just wasn't sure how to start.

When there were no tears left, I stood up and splashed some cold water on my face. I looked at myself in the mirror, piled my hair into a bun on top of my head, and willed myself to knit those two pieces inside of me into one.

I went back to my chair, set the pink glasses on the bedside table, further back this time so they wouldn't get knocked over again, and took Ansa's hand in mine.

"Thank you," I whispered, hoping she could hear me.

"I hope you get to see your daughter again.

I hope you get to hold her close, and I hope you get to be happy. When the stars are the only thing that we share, I wonder if you will still be there with me. I will remember your face, but not like this. I will remember your face with that mischievous smile, the scrunched-up nose making fun of me and nudging me towards Tessa. I wish you could see how royally screwed up I am making things, oh boy, you would be so mad. I wish I could ask a few more things… but I feel selfish. I want you to wake up for you too, I know how much dying with dignity meant to you. I wish I could have stopped them from doing all this to you. I wish I could have done more. But I threw the pills down the sink, Ansa, I did that. Just now. I'm not looking behind me anymore, I promise. I want you to know that. You did that. You saved me."

There was a small cough at the door. I hadn't realized I was talking out loud or that I was still crying.

"Do you want me to come back a little later?" Tessa asked. I noticed she had two coffees in her hands.

I smiled through the tears, a real smile that seemed to take her by surprise.

"No." I got up, grabbed the coffees and put them on the shelf outside the door, and then wrapped her in a tight hug.

"I am so sorry," I mumbled into her curly hair.

"Don't be, I can't even imagine what you are going through," she whispered.

"Yes, you can. You see this all the time, every day, and yet you still show up for the people that need you. Not just me, but these everyone here. You are a walking miracle, you are amazing," I said.

"You barely know me," she said laughing.

"Okay, I deserved that," I said, hugging her tighter, before pulling away. "I need to tell you some stuff."

"Me too," she said.

"Well, it's a good thing that there is coffee

then." I grabbed the cups and we both settled on the two cots that were not quite touching but close enough that we usually fell asleep holding hands.

"You go first," I said.

"Okay." She sipped on her coffee first and adjusted the plaid blanket so it covered her folded legs.

"We have raised the money to keep my job, but what if I want more?"

I laughed. "More money? Tess, I don't think we can get much more out of these people for just my rusty piano playing."

"No, no, not more money. More for myself. More than this." She motioned to her surroundings.

"I thought you loved what you do?"

"I do, I absolutely do. But I don't think I will ever really be seen here as anything but a wasted paycheque by the corporate side of things."

She definitely had a point. We had talked about the suits for many hours with Ansa. Ansa had worried even with the money that the same thing would happen when it came budget time next year. We had seen them around the floor lately, making changes and clearly not anticipating the benefit show to make any changes in their ultimate budget planning.

"So what does wanting more mean for right now?" I asked.

"Well, technically we are raising money for hospice care, under my name. The money goes directly to me. What if we take it elsewhere?"

I was about to ask a million more questions, but she put her hands up and grabbed a notebook under her cot.

She handed me a real estate listing.

"It's on the other side of Whitegate, used to be a physiotherapy clinic so it has the right kind of setup."

"You want to buy a house?" I think the shock was evident on my face.

"No, I want to buy a home. A hospice home,

one that caters to end of life needs, not just medical but everything under the moon. I want to take Lorraine with me; she can be the charge nurse and I can run the place, and I can hire people like myself, people who are underappreciated but who love what they do with every fiber of their being. People who want better for these friends of ours, people who remember what it was like to be in that bed and who wished they had something to distract them from the pain. Something to think of other than the end."

She caught her breath and looked at Ansa in the bed.

"I want to call it Rainbow Bridge," she said, looking back at me, eyes full of hope.

"You amaze me." It was all I could manage, but it was the truth.

"Do you think we can do it?" she whispered, and I realized that for some reason she needed my validation.

"I think you can do anything you set your

mind to," I said. I watched her whole face relax as she leaned back on her palms, her eyes closed, a smile on her face.

"Hey," I said, "what did you mean about remembering what it was like?"

"I had cancer when I was twelve. Things came close. I was actually in this exact room, ironically, but I got another chance at life."

I had no idea, but it somehow made me love her even more. How can someone who had been through so much, at such a young age, still be motivated to help those around her?

"What kind of cancer?" I asked.

"Leukemia. It hung in there, but I kicked its ass in the end." She sipped her coffee again, and I couldn't help but laugh at how casual she said it.

"So you really think it could happen?" she asked again.

"I mean Lorraine may take some convincing, she's a tough nut to crack."

Tessa laughed at this. "She wants people to think that, but in reality she's as soft as a down-filled pillow. She won't have any other choice but to come with me, and I think some of the other nurses and care aides are fed up with the management here too. If they don't want to be patient centered, and they don't want to listen to us, we'll just take the patients with us. Look at the back of the page, look at the backyard."

"Wow," I said, turning it over.

It had a large amount of property surrounding the two-storey building. You could see White-gate Bay; you could walk through the water, and you could sit under the stars and dance in the rain. It was so quaint, yet it was full of emotion. It reminded me of home, back in BC where we would have Pow Wows. I wondered if I would start to feel a connection with my ancestors being close to the water. I thought about how much I loved to take that route home from work, where I could smell the salty air and breathe in the earth.

"Have you looked into permits?"

She nodded, and I sipped my coffee. She already knew how I liked my coffee, and if that wasn't the start of a beautiful relationship, I didn't know what was.

"We already have enough to get started, money wise. We can do a down payment on the place and get all our operating licences and permits. We would have to get a palliative care team in the place, that would be the biggest outset cost, but there are a few doctors here I can make a pitch to take on a small caseload of patients at a new hospice. There are options."

I leaned over and kissed her, placing a hand on the small of her back and pulled her body towards mine. She was a wonder.

"I think those are amazing options. I think Ansa, Herb—hell, *everyone* would agree that you deserve so much more." I rested my forehead on hers, our eyes closed, content to be together.

"What did you want to tell me about?" she asked. I opened my eyes and shifted away from her.

"I need help, professional help." It was hard to say, but I managed the words through the tightness in my throat.

"What do you mean?" she asked, her eyes wide.

"I have a problem; I'm depressed and addicted to pills. Wow," I laughed, shocked. "I have never said that out loud to another person outside of the emergency room, I'm starting to feel nauseous."

"That's where I met Ansa. In the emergency room. It was the two-year anniversary of my mother's death and I tried to kill myself—I think meeting Ansa saved me."

I felt tears brimming in my eyes, I wanted to be better for her, but I knew that there were still refills for my pills back at the loft and I knew I needed to find a way to cope with those momentary reflexes of wanting to disappear into the great beyond.

"I'm sorry—I understand if this changes things," I said and braced myself for the blow about to come.

"Oh Caspar." She took my hand. "I love you. I'm not perfect either, nobody is. That's the first thing you learn around here, we all have regrets and we all want to be better. The first step is admitting you have a problem, the second step is asking for help. Needing help is not a bad thing, okay?" She wiped a tear from my cheek with her sweater sleeve, and then lifted my chin up so I was looking at her instead of the floor.

"I don't want to lose you; do you understand that?" she asked.

"I don't want to lose you either."

"Well, I guess that settles that," she said.

"I almost took some today, for the first time in months. When you went to get coffee," I admitted.

She didn't say anything, but I appreciated the

silence more than any words.

I continued, "But I knocked her glasses off the table, and I thought about her and you, and then I poured them all down the sink."

She cringed, and I thought she was about to say I was too much to handle, but instead she just pursed her lips and said, "so next time, we will make sure to consider the fishes, okay?"

I felt weight leave my shoulders when she laughed. It felt like I had confided in someone who truly understood, who didn't just scold me for throwing away what I did have going for me, or who tried to say they understood which seemed so utterly inconceivable.

"Can I help you find someone to talk to?" she asked quietly.

"I think I would like that," I said.

"You can talk to me too, of course. But I'm going to be here as your girlfriend at the end of the day." She realized what she had said, and I saw her face flush red.

"Girlfriend, huh?" I brushed a strand of hair out of her face, tucking it behind her ear.

"I mean, romantically involved partner without a label of some sorts?" She cringed in embarrassment.

"I prefer girlfriend, if I'm honest." I leaned in and kissed her again.

"I have an idea," I said.

"Okay?" she said suspiciously, fighting the smile on her face. She was so beautiful.

I left the room and walked to the nurse's station; I never liked using the call bell unless there was an actual emergency. I knew the nurses were busy handling emergencies all over the place and I didn't feel right calling them for things that weren't urgent.

Lorraine sat behind the computer and eyed me up as she always did. It was like she wanted to like me, but since she had to make up some story about who I was—a next of kin not on the paperwork is very suspicious— she always looked at me like I was about to cause trouble.

"Hi Lorraine, how are you this afternoon?" I asked with a smile.

"Fine, what can I do for you or your grandma?" Okay, I deserved that, and her gaze softened as she started to snicker at my uncomfortable grimace.

"I was wondering if we can bring Ansa to the lobby," I blurted, as if saying it faster gave me a better chance of agreement.

"Impossible. She is not stable enough, it's too risky." Lorraine looked back at the computer.

I was about to press the matter, but she was reading something on the screen, so I turned away and started back towards the room. Maybe another time, maybe she would wake up and we could go there without all the monitors and machinery.

"Wait," she said, not loudly, but I was straining for anything. I turned around and looked at her, full of hope.

"Is it for the piano?" she asked.

I nodded.

"We can't bring her to the lobby, but—"

"We can bring the piano to her!" I was running back to the room before finishing the sentence, calling over my shoulder. "You're a genius, Lorraine!"

I heard her laugh; maybe she didn't despise me after all.

CHAPTER TWENTY-SIX

Tessa

I brought all the patients on the floor to the advanced showing which was put together in the span of just a few hours.

I watched Caspar take the keyboard from our small activity room. He said it wouldn't sound the same as the grand piano, but then he kissed me and said the sound didn't matter—what mattered was the feeling people got when listening.

I was so in love with him, falling so fast and hard.

I knocked on all the patients' doors, not in uniform, technically not an employee, but it didn't matter. They all wanted to come to hear the music.

Even grumpy Marge, who was starting to get less grumpy as her days became more difficult to get through.

"Marge, do you want to come listen to some music?" I asked quietly as I walked into her room. Her eyes were closed and she was lying in bed.

"I haven't seen you in a while." She coughed a bit, and I went over to offer her some water from the cup on her table. She sipped on the straw and thanked me.

"There have been some budget cuts…"

"People think I'm crazy around here, but I am just angry. I'm allowed to be angry, am I not?" She grabbed my hand and started to cry.

"Of course, you are, Marge. You are allowed to feel however you want." She returned the smile I gave her.

"You know, I think I would like to listen to the music," she said while wiping the tears from her face.

I never prodded, that was always my rule. People shared what they wanted to share. I didn't know much about Marge, but I knew that there was more to her story, and she was the author of her life. I was only a reader of the last chapter, and who was I to say whether she let me read the rest? Some people were open books and wanted to be asked questions. But there were lots of people like Marge too, who just wanted peace and quiet and a comfortable ending to their days.

I wanted Rainbow Bridge to accommodate all wishes. I wanted to help the Herb's, the Ansa's, and the Marge's of the world to make sure that everyone ended their life in the way that they wanted. Surrounded by people who love them, surrounded by music, by nature, by friends, or by absolute nothingness. We would make it work, whatever they wanted, not the other way around.

I helped Marge into her wheelchair and brought her into the hallway where the care team was helping me to gather folks around the keyboard, and where Caspar sat just outside of Ansa's room.

She turned around to look at me and placed her hand on mine.

"Chase love. I let it slip away, and now I'm alone," she whispered.

"You're never alone, Marge." I squeezed her hand.

"I suppose not, but I feel alone. I just wish I had sought out more than work. I gave everything to a real estate company that barely could afford to let me retire, and then before I knew it, it was too late to do much of anything else with, or for, myself. The budget cuts may not be a bad thing, we all know how they treat you."

"You know Marge, I may have something you could help me with after the show, if you are interested?" I needed help figuring out how I would go through the down payment process—we couldn't afford a top-of-the-line real estate agent—but above all else, maybe it was something that would give her some fulfillment.

She smiled and laughed. "I don't know that there is anything this old lady can do for you, but sure I can try."

I smiled and patted her shoulder before leaving to gather some more patients. So many smiles and memories were in this building, but at the end of the day that's all it was—a building. I could take those memories and make new ones somewhere else, somewhere I could make sure that the patients always came first.

When all the patients were gathered in the small space, it felt warmer. I loved that feeling of bringing them all together and seeing them chat amongst themselves. I loved getting to be the person who brought them conversation, friendships, and something to do to pass the time. I remember wishing as a kid that the therapy dogs could stay forever, that the visiting therapy clowns would stay a little longer. I remember being afraid when there was nothing else to think about other than the reaper in the closet. Thankfully, I had my parents at my side, but for people like Marge, for people who didn't have anyone at their bedside, I often thought about them the most. I couldn't imagine what it would be like to live with that fear in your mind without any time away from it.

I went to find Caspar, as he had left the keyboard and was in the room talking to Ansa.

"You know, I think you'll recognize the first song. You actually inspired most of the show, well, you and my mum. I think you would both love it. I hope you can hear it; I hope you can hear me; I hope you know I'm still here…" He touched his forehead to her hand.

"Almost ready?" I asked quietly.

He sat up straight and smiled at me. "You look beautiful."

I had changed into one of the bright dresses I had packed in my duffel bag, I didn't want the patients to see me in my grey trackpants and hooded sweatshirt—it just was not the person they knew me to be, and it wasn't the person they needed either. I waved a hand as if to tell him nonsense but felt the butterflies in my stomach flutter.

He walked over to me and lifted me off the ground in a hug, spinning us around just like we had danced that night before it all changed.

"Do you think she can hear us?" he asked as he set me back on the floor.

"Absolutely I do." I smiled with conviction and led him outside to the crowd awaiting.

"Hi everyone! Thanks for coming out to our sneak preview of the concert happening in just a few weeks, on August 2nd." I paused and everyone applauded and cheered, even Lorraine was mixed in with the nurses and care aides who had paused from their business to enjoy the moment.

"This is my friend, Caspar." One of the care aides whistled, and Lorraine nudged her, "Okay, my boyfriend, Caspar."

Now there was an eruption of cheers, and even Marge smiled and winked at me.

"Anyhow! He is a renowned pianist and will be giving us a special glimpse into what we will be hearing at the benefit show." I looked over my shoulder and saw him stretching his hands, doing the physio exercises Ansa had made him do.

"So without further ado, here is the Rainbow Bridge show." The words tumbled out as naturally as they had seemed, and nobody batted an eye.

But my chest felt like it would implode with happiness, as I looked around the room and realized that I could use my voice, I could sing a song to my own drumbeat, and I vowed to make more memories. I could not be stopped; I would not be stopped.

I caught Marge staring at me, watching and waiting, and I felt like she could read my thoughts.

But my head was just an echo of words a friend had shared with me.

Words of wisdom were shouting through my head as I heard Caspar start to play, and the music carried my thoughts away—fired up on adrenaline about the prospect of being a ray of light in the lives of many, with no clouds in sight, and able to shine as brightly as I wanted to.

'Promise me, that you will keep true to who your heart tells you to be. Ignore everything else, that's where I went wrong.'

I would listen. With every fiber of my existence, I would listen to Herb.

'Nothing else matters when you are here, not a damned thing can come with you. So just, just listen to what your heart wants at all costs.'

My heart was telling me to follow my dreams, to follow the beat of my heart as it tugged me towards the real estate listing shoved in my pocket.

'Here I go.'

Me too, Herb, me too. I remember.

I would go with my heart instead of thinking about the risks. Because that seemed to be a constant thing around here, everyone had regrets but the one everyone seemed to have revolved around not following your heart. So I would follow mine, and I would hope for the best. After all, isn't that all we can really do in this life? Fighting against your heart is just counterproductive.

I sat next to Marge and enjoyed the rest of the show. The music carried me away, though, to Rainbow Bridge.

Charlie was at my side, and so was Caspar. We sat under the stars next to the water and planned the beginning of the journey. We would live together in a small house down the street, near the water because Charlie loves to swim. I wondered if Caspar liked the water; I still felt like I had so much more to discover about him, and about living, and I was grateful for the opportunity.

Caspar played the piano like he had never been injured, at least to me, someone who was not musically talented in the slightest. I was in awe of the way his hands moved over the keys with such precision and speed, never missing a note. I watched as his eyes met my own and a smile came to his face; I wondered if he knew how amazing he was. I watched as he looked at the faces of all the patients and wished I knew what was going through his head when he saw the way they looked at him.

I hoped he knew how appreciated he was.

His glance settled on Ansa in her bed in the room directly across from where he sat. I saw him close his eyes and finish the final song as he bowed his head and his hands rested in his lap.

Forty-five minutes had passed like the blink of an eye and there was a moment of silence as everyone registered the beautiful compositions they had heard. Then there was applause and the nurses cheered, the patients along with them. Lorraine was trying to hide her tears, but I saw them before she wiped them away and went back to work.

Caspar got up and bowed. He looked like he didn't know what to say and looked to me for help. When I got to him, I took his hand in my own. It was warm from playing.

"Thank you everyone for joining us for a special evening, we are excited to have you all there when we do the official Rainbow Bridge benefit show in the community garden," I said. Everyone clapped again, the applause quieting down as the nurses started ushering people back to their rooms.

"I have to go sit with her," Caspar said.

"Go, be with her. I'll be there shortly. That was incredible." I gave him a quick kiss before shooing him away.

Marge was still sitting in the foyer, watching me and smiling. A care aide went to move her wheelchair, but I stopped her.

"It's okay, I will bring her back." I smiled at the young girl, and she moved on to the next patient she had to return to their bed.

"He's special," she said over her shoulder as I brought her back to her room.

"Definitely."

I helped her back into bed; she had gotten a lot weaker over the last little while. Her dinner tray sat untouched, and I noted she had lost a substantial amount of weight.

"You want me to warm any of this up?" I asked.

"No, thank you." She shook her head. "I'm not eating much these last few days, it just comes right back up."

"Maybe they can give you a Gravol or something?" I suggested, worried about her.

She laughed and waved her hands at my worrying. "Enough about me, I am dying. Now, what did you want my help with?"

"Rainbow Bridge," I answered immediately.

She looked at me intensely. "If you want me to do some sad speech at your little musical show, count me out."

Marge could be so funny.

"Rainbow Bridge is a project of mine, not just a concert. It's a place."

She watched me closely, not saying anything, as I took the crumpled paper out of my pocket and smoothed it out before handing it to her. She adjusted the glasses on her small nose and squinted at the paper, reading through the whole thing. I couldn't read her face; maybe she had played professional poker in her life, because she had a damn good poker face.

She handed the paper back to me, abruptly pushing it into my hands.

"So?" I asked.

"You're crazy," she said, and folded her arms.

I looked at her and wondered if I was making a mistake even bothering her, since she had always seemed to be the type of lady who wanted to be left alone. But there was a glimpse of something else inside of her, something that made me want to get to know her more, something that felt unsaid.

"I like crazy," she said, with a sly smile.

"You had me for a second there, Marge," I sighed.

"Oh, I know!" she said, laughing.

"Will you help me figure out the real estate stuff?" I asked.

"Of course, although I may be a bit rusty. Do you have enough for the down payment that they are asking for?"

"Yes, the show raised enough money," I said, and she looked at me with pride.

"You're not using the money to stay here then?" she asked.

"How did you know about that?" I countered.

"I may not say much to anyone, but I am always listening."

I nodded my head. "I just—"

"Don't explain. Your reasons are your own. Never feel like you have to explain yourself to anyone but yourself."

I nodded my agreement, and she continued, "I will try to get it down in asking price, 25% below we will aim for—then you have more start-up money. You'll need a business account, have you got any of that setup?"

I shook my head, and she groaned. "You are going to have to get me a coffee and a computer."

"Absolutely," I said. "You got it, boss."

She narrowed her eyes at me, and I put my hands up in defence.

I left to check on Caspar and to gather the requests for Marge. Time was limited on our project; I wanted to announce it at the end of the show because I wanted people to know their money was going to have a larger impact. Another part of me wanted to watch the expression on the suits' faces as they heard I was leaving on my own terms.

Just as Ansa had wanted.

I sighed and was almost out the door when I

heard Marge whisper, maybe to me, maybe to herself, "thank you."

I smiled to myself and continued out the door.

CHAPTER TWENTY-SEVEN

Ansa

"You know, I think you'll recognize the first song. You actually inspired most of the show, well, you and my mum.. I think you would both love it. I hope you can hear it; I hope you can hear me; I hope you know I'm still here…"

I did know, and I could hear. Actually, I could hear better than when I was conscious. It was like I had lost all other senses and only my ears were still present on Earth. I felt pressure against my hand, and warmth along with it.

"Almost ready?" a female voice asked from further away.

The warmth left my hand, and I heard Caspar

say, "You look beautiful."

I missed my husband. I could hear him telling me those exact words, I could hear him telling me to come home to him, to let go. But I wanted to do this on my own terms, and I wanted to let Caspar know how he had saved himself. I needed him to know that he would be okay, I needed to tell him the things I didn't get the chance to tell Elena before it was too late.

"Do you think she can hear us?" I heard Caspar ask her quietly, also further away now.

"Absolutely I do," Tessa answered. I wanted to hug her so badly. I wanted to thank her for understanding, for knowing that I was still here, and for comforting him as well.

And then I could hear him playing. I knew it was him, because it was the same song we had played together when I was the strong one between the two of us, when he was too afraid to take the plunge and put his hands on the keys. It seemed like years ago that we had been at the piano in the lobby; I wondered if that's where we were. I wanted to open my eyes so badly, but I seemed to have forgotten how to do so.

I was cold, but I felt the weight of blankets against my body. It was a cold that came from the inside though. It's like there was frost forming on my bones. I wanted to music to come closer and wrap me in a warm embrace to shield me from that feeling. Instead, I felt the music carry me into sleep again.

When the music stopped, he came back in the room and held my hand. I could hear him talking to me, telling me that was an advance viewing of the show. I could hear him tell me about how I inspired the songs, and I heard sniffles coming from him as he told me that he loved me. I knew I couldn't respond; it was like I was in a cocoon.

I hoped that he wouldn't cry for too long, and I cursed the fact I couldn't tell him that for myself as I willed myself to speak, the words never finding their way to my lips.

I was getting ready for my ending, but I wanted to still be a part of the narrative.

I wanted to end my story before the ink ran out.

I would fight for that.

CHAPTER TWENTY-EIGHT

Caspar

That night we stayed up into the late hours of the night. Tess told me all about the conversations she had with Marge, and the look of hope in her eyes brought warmth to my chest. I was happy to be a part of her future. I was proud of her for making these tough decisions because I knew how much this place meant to her and how many memories she had here.

"You are an amazing pianist," she said, looking up at the ceiling, both of us waiting for sleep to come.

"And you are an amazing person," I said, turning my head so I could stare at her.

She looked at the plain ceiling like it was a

sky full of stars, her eyes brimming with optimism and hope. I smiled and closed my eyes.

"Would you move in with me?" she asked, and I bolted up into a sitting position.

"*What*?"

"Would you?" she looked at me calmly, reading my face.

"If that's what you want—but don't you think it's a little… fast?"

"Well, it has to be what you want too, but I don't know. We could get struck by lightning you know?"

"How optimistic of you," I said, laughing.

She flicked my shoulder lightly. "What I mean is, life moves so fast. I love you; I feel like I've known you for years, I want to get to know you better, and I don't want to waste time."

"I want that too. Can we at least wait a few months before adopting twins though?"

"I was thinking triplets, but sure."

We were silent for a few moments, then I felt her body press into mine. She was so warm, like a furnace. She fit like a missing puzzle piece, between my arms and into the crooks of my body.

We both woke up to the sound of violent coughing. I shot out of bed and went to the call bell. I pushed it maybe ten times and watched in horror as Ansa went from red to blue in colour, I switched the lights on above the bed, which only made the situation look worse. I was suddenly dry-heaving, and Tessa was shouting something into the hallway.

Tessa ran a hand over my back and pulled me away from the bed. There was so much commotion with nurses running into crowded room and machines beeping and screaming. It was a stark contrast to the most peaceful sleep I had just woke up from. It was like a nightmare.

Suddenly, I was on the bathroom floor, head in the toilet with my guts spilling out. Tessa held my hair behind my head, whispering it would be okay, telling me she was here, but all I could hear was the nurses shouting words I did not understand, and sentences that brought fear into my mind.

"What time is it?" I asked. I have no idea why.

"Just about six in the morning," she said, and I leaned my head against her knees.

She propped me up against the wall, and I closed my eyes and willed Ansa to fight. I wanted to talk to her so badly, I *needed* to talk to her again.

Tessa went to the sink and put cold water on some paper towels before pressing them to my forehead and the back of my neck.

"You're in shock, Caspar, just take a minute and focus on your breathing."

I listened to her and stared into her eyes. She offered a weak smile, but it was enough to distract me from the sounds outside of the washroom. She took me into her arms, joining me on the cold bathroom floor and holding the damp pieces of paper against my skin. I realized I was covered in sweat, my heart racing like it was sprinting a marathon, my vision was dark and blurry like I was going through a tunnel, and my legs were shaking.

I leaned my head against her chest and listened to her steady heartbeat.

I tried to focus on the sound of her heart beating and make mine match hers.

I focused on taking deep breaths in and out, and eventually I felt like I could breathe normally again.

There were still sounds outside of the washroom, but it sounded much less hectic. I looked at the door, terrified but knowing I had to find out if Ansa was alright. Then I realized I may have run away when she needed me most. I should have stayed there, holding her hand as she passed. I started to sob.

"Tess," I choked out through the tears, "can you go see if it happened?"

She nodded and placed a kiss on my clammy forehead before quickly slipping out of the washroom, closing the door behind her. I leaned my head against the cold wall and let the tears flow freely.

She was back in a few minutes, or maybe it was longer. I wasn't sure of anything anymore.

"Caspar, it's okay, she's okay," she said, with tears running down her face.

"What?"

Tessa smiled at me, brilliant and wide.

"She woke up. Caspar, Ansa woke up."

"No, I heard her choking, I heard her gasping for air." I didn't believe it; I couldn't believe it.

"She was choking on the feeding tube, she must have woken up and gotten confused and scared, it happens when someone wakes up suddenly," she said.

I sat there, head against the wall, and the sobs turned to laughter. I was laughing, while tears were still streaming down my face.

She sat next to me and pulled me close.

"I thought that was it," I said, "I really did."

"So did I," she agreed.

"Is she awake now?"

Tessa shook her head no. "They had to sedate her to remove the tubes properly, but she should be awake in a couple hours."

We stayed like that for a while, and then I realized I still had vomit on my clothes and was drenched in sweat.

"I think I'll take a quick shower," I said and squeezed Tessa's hand in my own.

"Are you okay to stand?" she asked.

"One way to find out, I guess." I started to get up and my knees felt heavy. "Just have to go slowly."

She helped me get steady on my feet and got my clothes out from my backpack for me. She even turned the shower on and laid a towel out, and I watched in sheer embarrassment as she pulled a fresh pair of boxers out of my bag, but she didn't seem to care, she was too focused on making sure I was alright.

"We should do it soon," I said suddenly.

"Do what?" she asked, distracted, as she put her hand in the water to see if it was warm enough.

"Let's move in together, sooner rather than later."

She spun around, eyes wide. "Really?"

"Really," I said. I never felt more confident in anything I had said before.

She wrapped her arms around my neck, and I took a deep breath of her. She was amazing, and I wasn't about to waste any more time. With anyone.

"I'll be right out," I said, as she opened the door and grinned at me one more time before leaving me to myself. I felt like my brain was on fire, so many thoughts flooding through my mind and leaving me in awe of being alive.

One moment, I was on the floor in sheer terror, losing control of my body, the next moment I was elated at the fact Ansa was awake and Tessa was by my side.

I peeled the dirtied clothes from my body, and stepped into the warm water of the shower, letting it wash away any part of the panic attack that remained. I found myself thinking of my mother, wondered what she would think of the man I had turned into. When she left me, I was a boy. I had grown so much, so fast, that I was unsure of how she would react. I think she would've loved Tessa, though. I was sad that they were never going to meet—at least in this lifetime. But I smiled at the thought of my mom watching over us until that happened.

The water cascaded over me, washing away any bad feelings. My mother would love that I decided to grow my hair out, just like how my fathers was, and his father before that and so on. I twisted my hair and wrung out some of the water.

Hair was seen as a source of power and strength in Indigenous culture. It held a special spiritual and cultural significance amongst tribes, though traditions and styles vary from tribe to tribe. My mother would always tell me growing my hair long would bring me closer to Mother Earth whose hair is long grasses. I remember seeing photos of my mother with short hair. When I was old enough, she told me about cutting all her hair off when my dad passed away, which symbolized the time she spent with him, letting him go from Earth and allowing new life to grow within herself. She told me about going to the reserve and watching the Elders burn her locks of hair and her extended family holding her hand as she cried throughout the ceremony.

When she passed away, I contemplated doing the same. But when I thought about losing the hair she once brushed through, or braided for me when I was a boy, all I could do was cry.

So I let it grow, longer than ever before. And I thought of her every time I braided it or put it in a bun atop my head.

When I changed into the clothes Tessa had laid out for me, I realized it was the outfit I was wearing when we first kissed that night in the rain and wondered if it was intentional.

I walked out of the washroom, hair still damp and dripping water onto the nape of my neck where it was braided to my lower back. Tessa sat in the chair next to the bed, and I pulled another one next to it. There was so much empty space in the room now, it was comforting to see the absence of most of the monitors and wires coming from the bed. Instead, it was just a pale Ansa, who looked like a shell of herself. I didn't think it was possible for bones to protrude in that way from your face. She looked malnourished and the sight of her made me ache.

"She may not have long, Caspar," Tessa whispered, grasping my hand.

I nodded and appreciated her telling me the truth.

We sat in silence for the rest of the morning;

every time Ansa stirred, both of us bolted upright in our chairs.

And then, at 9:05 in the morning, her eyes fluttered open.

I grabbed for her hand, and Tessa grabbed for the call bell. We were both on our feet instantly.

Ansa just stared at us, bewildered. She tried to open her mouth, but all that came out was a cough. She winced in pain, her eyes struggling to stay open.

"It's okay, don't try to talk just yet," Tessa said.

"Don't talk yet, Ansa, we are here," I said, and then I reached for the pink glasses on the bedside table and put them on her face as gently as I could. I tucked a strand of her hair behind her ear and watched in amazement as she managed to bring a smile to her face.

"Is she awake?" It was Lorraine, before her shift, civilian clothes on and purse over her shoulder.

Tessa nodded and ushered her into the hallway, they chatted for a few moments while I stayed in the room with Ansa. We were just staring at each other, holding hands.

Time stood still. To see her smiling at me, however weak, was more than I could have asked for.

And then Lorraine was back, checking different monitors and writing things on her palm. I learned that nurses always used their skin as paper. Then she reached for the cup of thickened fluid that the care aides had brought in for when Ansa woke up.

"Well, good morning sunshine. You gave us all a fright," she said, as she offered Ansa the straw. "Drink, it'll help soothe your throat. It may be hard to talk for the first little bit."

Ansa nodded, and when she finished her drink, she managed to croak a hoarse, "Thank you."

Tessa and I exchanged an excited glance, Ansa saw both of us and a smile appeared again on her face.

Lorraine looked between me and Ansa. "We have to have some difficult conversations, Ansa, but you let me know when you are ready. I'm sorry to bring this up right now, but I know how much you had wanted to go on your own terms—you may not have a lot of time to make that decision now, so just call for me when you are ready to chat, okay?" She said it like she didn't want to have to, and for that I felt like I could see Lorraine's heart on her sleeve.

Ansa nodded, and reached for Lorraine's hand.

I saw the look in her eyes, as she looked at Ansa and smiled. In that moment, I understood why her and Tessa got along so well.

Before she left, she patted my shoulder and gave Tessa a quick hug.

And then it was the three of us once again. Maybe not for long, but at least we had each other, for one small moment.

I thanked Mother Earth, something I had not

done since my mother had passed.

CHAPTER TWENTY-NINE

Ansa

I felt like I had swallowed gravel and had been tram-pled on by boxing day shoppers at the local super-store.

I was getting ready for my ending, but I want-ed to still be a part of the narrative.

I wanted to end my story before the ink ran out.

I had fought for that.

My body felt like I had physically fought a battle; I wouldn't be surprised if someone held up a mirror and showed me missing teeth, hair pulled out, and bruises all over my frail body.

The image before me though was the man

who was not the boy he had been just a few months ago in the emergency room. I was not sure what had changed, though I had an idea, but that boy was no longer there. Then there was the woman with the fire in her heart and on her head, the woman who looked at me like I was the best friend she ever had. She was burning even brighter than before.

I realized then that their story was just beginning. What would be my epilogue would be their opening credits.

Caspar held my hand and stared at me as though I would leave him any second, as though the words he wanted to say were lodged in his throat and the tears that brimmed his eyes were daggers threatening to slice through skin.

"Boo," I managed to croak.

A sigh of relief came from them as they grinned at me, and squeezed my hands. A tear fell from Caspar's eyes.

"I didn't think I would get to talk to you

again, I wasn't sure, I thought…" Caspar took a deep breath, his eyebrows bunched together in sorrow.

"What do you mean, child?" I asked.

His silence remained, the only sound in the room was the whine of the air conditioning unit underneath the window and the muted chatter and squeaking shoes coming from the hallway.

I looked at them both and tried to bring a smile to my face even though the act of doing so felt like moving a mountain with my bare hands.

"I heard you all along, I was with you the whole time, boy," I said.

He hung his head, and we stayed in silence for what felt like hours. The clock on the wall told me it was only minutes, but time had seemed to slow for me since I was back here. I found myself wanting to go back to sleep, as much as I was happy to have been given even a few more moments. My body was so tired.

I shifted under the blankets, and Tessa was

there instantly, helping me to readjust.

"Thank you," I said, "both of you, for everything."

Caspar looked at me, and I could tell he wanted to say so many things but was struggling to put the words together. Tessa looked between us and then excused herself for the restroom, but I watched her knowingly. She was giving us some time, giving *him* some time, and I think it was just another reason why I knew he would be okay. I think she was exactly what he needed, someone who understood that even though she wanted to help him get through his problems, he would still need to stand up on his own. She could help him, but she couldn't do it for him.

She was gone for a few minutes before I coughed, and Caspar helped me drink some of the thickened gelatin like fluid.

"You know I won't be here for long?" I asked. I had to make sure he knew.

"I know, and I know what it means to you to

have some say in it," he paused and ran his hands over his knees, "I just don't understand."

"I don't think any of us really do," I said, and meant it. More silence followed, but I had an idea.

"I want to go out to look at the stars," I proclaimed, and his back stiffened.

"I don't know if that's allowed..." He looked at me as though I would break as soon as I moved a muscle, and it made me want to stay in bed for his sake, to not add any more stress than I had already.

But it's what I wanted.

"It'll be the last thing I see Caspar; I want the last thing I see to be the stars." I smiled, as the thought itself brought goosebumps to my arms. I wasn't afraid anymore, sometime between when I was last awake and now, I had found peace. I was thankful that my heart no longer feared what was to come.

Caspar just looked at me and nodded his head.

"It will be alright, my friendly ghost friend."

I wiggled my fingers and he reached for my hand.

Again, he nodded, but this time the look on his face was different. The pained expression on his face had smoothed, and he looked just as at peace as I was.

"You were really there all along, you heard everything?" he asked.

"Yes, every word. I heard you." I willed him to believe me, knew he needed to know. Knew he needed to know that if I heard him, there was a chance his mother did as well, knew that he needed to know that both of us loved him, and wanted him to have peace.

He just nodded his head and murmured, "Thank you."

I squeezed his hand, and pain flowed in my arm.

"Caspar…" I whispered, my vision blurring a bit.

"Do you need anything?" He was on his feet,

ready to do whatever I needed.

"Lorraine, will you get her for me please?"

He nodded, knowing the task at hand would contribute to the end of me, but his face was nothing but peace.

He turned on his heels, but I croaked, "Wait."

He looked back, a question on his face.

"You saved yourself, nobody else could have ever done that for you," I said.

I could see him try to fight back his tears, but he continued out of the doorway and Lorraine came in shortly afterwards to discuss next steps.

And then it was done.

Just like that.

I asked her if we could do it outside, somehow, if I could be outside and have my friends with me, and if the stars could be the last thing I saw.

I expected it to be hard to talk about, but instead I found myself so at ease with the idea of slipping away from the body that now felt more like a trap. I wondered why we assumed older people matched their body on the outside; I was still in here, it was the same me I had always been. Nothing had changed, except that my body had started to betray me.

I sighed a breath of relief when Lorraine told me she would make something work and wrapped me in a hug. She helped me sign my name, which I had to do repeatedly with the overwhelming amount of paperwork involved in having a doctor help you to end your suffering. I didn't like to think of it as killing myself, because I wasn't really. I was letting go of this body, sure, but I was still able to speak and breathe and think my own thoughts and something about that was a miracle in and of itself.

Instead, I thought of it as leaving this state of being. I had hope that I would see my family again, that I would be with them again and be able to finally tell them all the things I had held onto. It wasn't all tied to religion though, sure I was Hindu, but I found myself also just feeling as though I had faith in the universe, in myself, in the stars and the sky and the very fact that we even exist.

Perhaps it was deathbed shenanigans, but it felt like a real sense of divinity had wrapped itself around me.

We signed the last few papers, and Lorraine disconnected a few more cables and wrote another message on her palm. I wondered how she never ran out of space. Another hug, and a final verbal consent to contact the doctor and confirm scheduling, and she was off with a smile.

I was alone for a while then, just me and my thoughts and the evening approaching. Time had slowed this morning, but now it was marching steadily on towards eight o'clock when the needle was scheduled.

I wondered if Elena would be older now, wondered if we continued to age in the beyond, or if we were some sort of energy bubble—if we were the bubbles, would we all be different colours, would there even be colours?

This was deathbed shenanigans, I mentally scolded myself.

All that mattered, was that I was making the right choice for myself.

I told myself I would close my eyes just for a moment until they came back, but when I woke up next the stars were already there.

It was my time.

CHAPTER THIRTY

Caspar

It was the strangest night, the stars seemed to come out earlier just for her. The sun had barely disappeared behind the clouds when bright burning specks of white were already visible from where we were gathered in the garden.

I had pictured this moment, this entire day, being a lot different. I thought I would have so much to say, thought there was so much that we needed to talk about, but instead just getting to be in each other's presence, knowing she was okay and was making this decision on her own terms, seemed to bring peace into it for all of us.

When she told me she heard me all along, it

made me realize I wasn't as alone as I always seemed to think. Maybe my mother could still hear me too, maybe she was still with me sometimes, maybe she lived on through me, maybe I would see her again. And maybe Ansa had been right all along, maybe I had saved myself in the end.

Where some may think these potentials would cast a shadow of doubt in my mind, instead they brought a renewed sense of hope.

Ansa stirred, and we all crowded beside the bed, she struggled to open her eyes. When she did, a bright smile flashed across her face as she took in her surroundings. The sky had just started to darken, and the doctor had just arrived and was readying the medications inside.

I held her hand, and Tess held my other hand.

"Ansa?" I asked softly, afraid to disrupt the peaceful smile on her face.

She turned to look at me, and I was glad to have gotten the time I did have with her.

I felt tears come to my eyes, but not entirely made up of sadness.

"Don't cry, child." She smiled at me as if she understood every thought and feeling I was processing.

I wasn't sure how much time had passed; it was like the three of us were fixed in time and place. We kept staring into each other's eyes and it was like having the most intimate conversation inside of our heads, the most peaceful goodbye I had ever experienced.

The doctor came over and asked for consent again, and Ansa was only momentarily disturbed from our internal dialogue before she looked back at us and smiled.

Suddenly I felt words come to my mouth. "While our time together was short, only a dent in the universe's timeline… it will always be my small infinity."

I felt tears roll down my cheeks as I caught

sight of the doctor pushing the plunger of the needle down, and I felt Tessa's hand grip mine tighter.

I focused on the look on Ansa's face though.

Tessa brushed the hair out of Ansa's face and leaned in for a hug.

"You will always be our story," she whispered, not knowing I had heard.

I squeezed her hand too, and then we all looked at the stars.

"I was glad," Ansa said, breathing deeply, "to have been infinitely small with you both. To have felt the way living feels, and now, I will see you again in the stars."

It only took a few moments, she kept breathing slower and slower until there was one sharp inhale and she softly whispered, "Elena…" and her eyes widened.

Then her body relaxed underneath the blankets and her eyelids fluttered closed. I softly let go of her hand as the doctor came over to check for any signs of life before pronouncing the time of death.

And just like that, one story had ended.

Not her story, and not mine or Tessa's—but the one where all three of us came into each other's lives and thus found answers about the world around us, about the way things worked, the people we were, and the people we had become. That story had concluded, with a triumphant smile resting upon all our faces, with a soft breeze in the air, with a feeling of purpose in our hearts, and a renewed sense of self.

The stars seemed brighter that night, or maybe it was just the way I looked at them now that I knew she was amongst them.

The star with the pink glasses.

CHAPTER THIRTY-ONE

Tessa

The same night after Ansa had passed on, we sat in her empty hospital room for a while just staring at the walls. It was the thought of *what next?* that echoes through our skulls, and we were both uncertain until Caspar just stood up and started packing things into his backpack.

I sat on the cot on the floor, the space that had become our little home for the past few weeks, at the foot of a bed where there was nobody to connect our stories together anymore.

It was just us now. I felt tears start to fall down my face, and suddenly I was sobbing into my hands. I didn't usually feel the kind of loss I was feeling in that moment, and I think it caught me off guard because suddenly I was unsure of everything. I was unsure about my career, my relationship, my home. I wasn't sure what home meant anymore, because the last time I went to my parent's house I realized I felt more at home in this tiny space with a man I hardly knew, and a woman who was dying.

Caspar dropped his backpack; I heard the contents crash into the tiles. Then he was pulling my hands away from my face, kneeling in front of me. When I looked into his deep brown eyes, all I saw was love.

He smiled softly at me, wiping the tears from my face gently.

"What can I do?" he asked, looking in pain from seeing me breakdown. I don't think I had ever sobbed like this in front of someone, including people who I had known for years, and especially not in front of anyone as handsome as he was. I felt my face redden, and I shrugged my shoulders.

"I don't know," I answered.

"What's on your mind?" he asked and contin-ued to thumb away any tears that fell down my face, holding my gaze with such concern in his eyes.

"What happens next?" I could hardly breathe the words; they were like a cautious whisper.

"What do you want to be next?" he asked.

I took a minute to look around the empty room, it felt wrong to even be in here, and I felt my heart rate start to speed up like the beginning of a panic attack. I hadn't had one since grade school, but I wasn't about to turn tonight into anything about me. I realized the only thing I wanted to do.

"I want to go home," I said.

He stayed kneeling on the floor, waiting until the tears had stopped falling down my face.

Eventually, he asked, "Where is home?"

I breathed a laugh out, a small one, because it felt like we were playing a game of twenty questions at the worst time in the world. He stood up and held out his hand. I grasped it and stood beside him as we took in the empty room.

"With you," I said, finally.

A short while later, we had packed up the few things in Ansa's room which would serve as a memory and a reminder of the prologue in our story together, something neither of us knew at that point in time.

And then we were walking down the hallway and saying goodbye to the nurses, and I watched with a smile as Lorraine pulled a cautious Caspar in for a bear hug. When she decided she liked you, she loved you for life.

I realized this was the last time I was going to feel like this place was what made me who I was. I had gotten that wrong for so long; it's not our experiences that define us, it's how we react to them.

Lorraine already knew the contents of the envelope I handed to her. She only nodded her head before walking over to the scanner and smoothing the papers over the glass top and waving goodbye to us.

Caspar watched her, and then looked at me with raised eyebrows, but I simply shook my head. Today wasn't the day.

All that was left was to go home.

I had my duffel bag in hand, as well as another backpack filled with things from work that had accumulated over the years spent here. Caspar had a backpack on his back, and a bag of Ansa's things in his hand.

We stood in the lobby, by the piano, where we had some memories together and I had many with my parents in my early years. I willed a silent goodbye and felt Caspar's warm hand take hold of my own.

I nodded at him, and then pushed open the steel doors into the crisp air of the night.

It had just rained, the night sky back to shining brilliantly with thousands of stars already. It was as if it had a quick cry with us as well, but then remembered it had to get back to showing the world what wonders lied outside of our little bubbles.

"Should I call a cab?" he asked from beside me.

"No, I think I want to walk," I replied.

He nodded his head, and asked, "Do you need to go to your place first?"

I shook my head. "No, I have everything I need."

Even though I had no idea where he lived, when we turned the corner and I saw the cozy loft, I realized that had to be it. I looked between the stars, my hand entwined in his, and felt my heart pull me towards the cozy warmth of it.

"Sorry, it's probably a mess," he said.

"You've never seen my closet," I replied with a shrug and curiously watched as he led me up the stairs and jiggled the key in the lock.

It instantly felt like home; it was the same way he felt… like I had known him for years. It was small, a lot of people would have probably said it felt stuffy, but to me it felt like coming home after a long vacation.

I sat on the small couch in the living room area and laughed as he scurried around to tidy up. I saw him pause in the kitchen.

He was holding papers in his hand, and the look in his eyes went a lot deeper than any small tidying up task.

I went to stand behind him. "Are you okay?"

I placed my palm on his shoulder, and noticed he was holding a stack of prescriptions. I knew what he was trying to do and didn't have the words to say. Funny how you can go to school to be a social worker, you can find out how humans work and think, and then suddenly when you aren't at work, when you are living your life and the person you love needs that kind of help—nothing applies. No therapy technique works on someone you love.

All you can do is be there. So I stood with my

palm on his back for a few minutes, and watched as he ripped the papers in half. I couldn't imagine what he was going through, the thoughts going through his mind. I wrapped my arms around his waist and held him.

Suddenly, he turned around and wrapped his arms around my neck as well. It reminded me of that night we had danced together, while Ansa was still a part of our narrative. I felt a pang of grief in my chest, though I was happy that she had been there for any of it at all.

I think we forget how precious time with one another really and truly is until it is taken away from us.

"Now," he breathed and leaned his forehead against mine, "we can call it home."

We both stayed like that for a while before we remembered it was three in the morning. We went to bed, and just like that, it was the start of moving in together. The loft became home from the moment I walked through the door, or maybe even earlier.

At first, it was just a backpack's worth. I told my parents I was just going to stay with him to make sure he didn't do anything to hurt himself, especially with what he had been through, and I was worried about him. I didn't even fully believe the reasoning myself as I watched him rip up his prescriptions the night before. In truth, I didn't really know who we were without the connecting piece of the woman in the pink glasses with a heart of purest gold. I was afraid that if I let him out of my sight, I would lose him. I couldn't stand the thought of being away from him.

A few days later, it was a suitcase, and then the next day I asked for my dad to swing by and leave Charlie with us for a night or two. I think that was when they started to know it was going to be a permanent thing, so when they brought Charlie, we had them stay for dinner.

It didn't feel like an awkward 'meet my boyfriend over takeout' meal, it felt like Friday night at home. Wherever he was is where I felt at home.

"Thanks for coming over," I said at the door when my parents were leaving.

My mom's eyes were glimmering with un-shed tears. "I really like him, Tess," she whispered.

I stifled my laughter but felt myself blush; it meant a lot to me that they approved. I was close with them, and I couldn't imagine hurting them any-more than I had when I was a child, even if it was outside of my control. I knew what this must feel like, losing me all over again, and I wanted them to know I was still here.

It was a new chapter though; one I was ready to begin with too high a spirit to be encumbered by any of my yesterdays.

My dad broke the silence. "I hate to have to say it, but I agree with your mother, I like him, but he's got to prove he is worthy every time I see you guys, which I hope will be a lot."

I hugged them both, a family squished together. "Of course."

"We have fifty-fifty Charlie custody, understood?" my dad said sternly.

I burst into laughter and scratched Charlie behind the eras as he stood beside me on the porch, tail wagging against the wooden paneling.

"Understood," I said, with an army salute.

"And I get holidays!" he yelled, as my mom started to drag him back towards the truck. I could hear Caspar laugh from where he was sitting at the top of the stairs.

I shook my head and closed the door as they got into the car, laughing with one another.

I hoped we would be like them when we grew old together, I hoped we would laugh together like that always.

"I'm going to have to take him to court, aren't I?" I asked Charlie, bending down to kiss him on the head.

Caspar watched us from the top of the steps and smiled.

"Big day tomorrow," he offered.

"Is it?" Charlie had rolled over for belly rubs, and I obliged and looked playfully confused at him as he shook his head at me.

"Charlie, want to go for a walk?" Caspar boomed with excitement.

The W-word was Charlie's demise, he abandoned me like I was chopped liver, and went bounding up the stairs.

"That's not playing fair, now we have to actually go for a walk." I rolled my eyes at him.

He pulled the leash out from behind his back and grinned. Maybe introducing them was not such a great idea; I was starting to feel like the two of them had a better relationship than we did.

I got up from the floor, and we were on our way to the waterfront walking trail we had started to visit a few times a day.

We both realized the day we woke up after Ansa's death that while we knew the big things, we hardly knew anything miniscule about one another. So we called them Getting to Know You walks, and every question had to be answered with another question. It became a favourite pass time, and now that Charlie was here, I was sure they would only grow in popularity.

It felt like we were rewinding the tape, like we had tackled the big stuff first and now we were finding out about each other's pet peeves and favourite colours. We knew each other's deepest fears and secrets, but I had no idea he was from Canada.

His favourite colour was red; mine was green.

His favourite animals were eagles; mine were sharks.

He was an Aquarius; I was a Sagittarius. This fact intrigued me, I wondered if Ansa knew we were written in the stars literally.

I learned about his nine to five job and in response told him about how my career had started.

We spent every minute we had together getting to know one another, and at some point, it became clear that we were compatible. It was like we were afraid that our relationship was founded on nothing but adrenaline and raw emotions due to the complex scenario we found each other in. But then we realized that we would also be friends if we had met in line at the coffee shop, and that made everything feel just a bit more comfortable between us.

He held the leash in one hand, and my hand in the other.

I looked at him and smiled instantly.

"What?" he asked, blushing and laughing, squeezing my hand.

"I love you," I said.

"I know," he teased, "I love you too."

I could hear Herb in the back of my head, reminding me 'just, just listen to what your heart wants at all costs.' We continued our walk down the trail until the comforting scent of the water was tingling at my nose.

"I have to tell you something!" I remembered suddenly.

We were on the small shore now; Caspar had let Charlie off the leash and was finding a good stick to throw for him. He looked up from his hunt for the stick, and Charlie stared at me like I had ruined his fun, tongue lopped out of his mouth.

"Uh-oh," he mumbled.

"No, nothing bad—We have a change of venue for tomorrow!"

"We do?" he asked.

"Yes! And we also have a ribbon cutting ceremony."

I grabbed his wrist and dragged him to the small picnic table nestled next to the trees by the water. He grabbed a stick along the way and threw it into the water for an excited Charlie, who bounded in to retrieve his prize.

Caspar had told me he had never had a pet before, but from the way he looked at Charlie… I think he was in love with both of us now.

He sat across from me. "So what's the story?"

I laughed because it seemed there was always a story these days, it seemed like this was the biggest story of our life. I think we were both looking forward to the days where we could just enjoy a TV show and crappy takeout and fall asleep together on the couch.

"I quit my job, I bought the property, Marge helped, and we open in a few months."

His mouth dropped open.

That had all happened on the day Ansa had woken up and passed away, it was such a blur. I had left Caspar alone with Ansa, excusing myself to use the restroom, and then was gone for hours. I wanted them to have their time together because I knew they needed it.

I decided to keep my mind busy though, and

Marge and I got to work. We made so many phone calls, we sent so many emails, I told Lorraine everything and then when it was done. We had a timeline put together and everything, a lot of the waiting periods were dismissed because we were already certified in our fields respectively, and it wasn't technically an acute care centre, it was hospice. It was end of life care; it was a stopping point on people's journey into the beyond.

Four months and we would open our doors. We had the funding for staff, for opening costs, and for the down payment and first few mortgage payments. There were some additional licensing fees that Lorraine managed to work into our capital plan as well, and she somehow got me approved for a loan to cover these costs. I later came to find out she co-signed on the loans.

Lorraine agreed to join me in my quest, convincing her was much easier than I had anticipated it would be. She said she would go wherever at this point because she was so fed up with the politics at St. Bartholomew's.

Refer to the previous commentary about Lorraine. If she loves you, she loves you with everything she is.

But the one that came out of left field was when Marge asked, "Can I be your first patient? If I don't croak by then, that is?"

Lorraine and I looked between each other, and then grinned at the woman who so many—my dear friend Herb included—dismissed as bitter and uncaring.

She laughed when I told her, "Absolutely, you can even cut the ribbon."

Then I had written the letter to the suits. The same letter, which I had kept a copy of and now reached into my pocket for. I handed it to Caspar, the man I loved, that was now collecting flies with his unhinged jaw and state of small shock.

I smoother the crumpled paper, I had planned

on showing it to him over dinner, but when we had unexpected guests, the night had gotten away from me, and I nearly forgot to tell him about it.

I bit my lip and handed the paper to him.

To whom it may concern,

Please accept this letter as formal notice of my resignation from St. Bartholomew's Hospital, specifically my role as a Recreation Therapist on the Palliative Care Unit (PCU), effective immediately.

I have seen the PCU from both perspectives, a patient and an employee, and I can say with absolute truth, this was the hardest decision I have made in my life. I have been honoured to play a small role in the health and wellbeing of my patients for the past five years. I thought I would spend the entirety of my career here; however, when my position was put on the line and I realized that I would never been seen in your eyes as something of value, something worth fighting for, I decided it is what is best for myself and my future. Please know that I did not appreciate being made to fight for a job that you will soon realize (as I have been directing families to send complaints to your respective emails, hope you don't mind but you were never there in person for them to talk to), had a large impact on patients and their families alike.

You will also come to realize the discontent of your staff, as it was very easy to get the majority of them to help me with an upcoming project. Please know we are not abandoning our patients, we are simply thinking about future patients, and want to ensure that their wants and needs are properly listened to and advocated for, something which was made clear by your dissolution of my job, to not be possible within your domain.

I have held the hand of many, I have dried the tears of even more, I have helped the grieving families, the widowed spouses, the terrified newly diagnosed. I have seen a lot of grief and suffering, and yet what hurt the most was the sheer disrespect and carelessness towards the wellbeing of staff and patients that you have put on display.

What you may not realize is how important those art displays you tore down in the hallways were. They were something that reminded us of all the people we had lost. There were paintings on there that were done by people who passed away years ago, and you placed them in a trash receptacle.

I don't say any of this to make you feel ashamed, I truly wish you and the team at St. Bartholomew's the best. My hope instead is that there is a lesson somewhere between these lines, that this is a learning experience, that the corporate culture shifts and that you come to realize the importance of health in all aspects of personhood.

You can tear down the garden, but when you do, know that a man named Herb planted the tomatoes. He didn't think that they would grow, but within a month we were slicing one up to share amongst us. Oh, and the rocks in the garden are hand painted by a woman named Beth, she was only with us for a short time, but you can see what a bright spirit she had from the way she painted those rocks. The frog statue, I know it's a little ugly, but one of our patients named Henry donated it to the garden, it was one of the first gifts he ever bought for his wife, and she damn near called off their marriage!

There is a story behind everything—make sure you take the time to read it.

Sincerely,

Tessa Murphy, RSW, RRT
Registered Social Worker
Registered Recreation Therapist

**PS. the Benefit Show you graciously allowed me to put together to try and save my own career will no longer be hosted at St. Bartholomew's. Since the* *garden is being torn down, we decided to just move it to where the funds will actually be going—a new Hospice Care Centre in Whitegate, called Rainbow Bridge. Maybe I can drop off some flyers for you all to post before we open our doors?*

His mouth was still open a few moments later, when I was sure he had read through it at least two times, and Charlie had come to lay at our feet with his stick.

"So?" I asked expectantly.

"I am…" He lifted his palms up, expression blank.

I panicked. "I was going to tell you sooner, but then everything happened so fast, and it never felt like the right time. I am sorry, I should have told you sooner, I just thought…"

He was smiling at me.

"I am so proud of you!" He threw Charlie's stick again before he came over to sit next to me.

"You are?" I asked, dumbfounded.

"Hell yes, Tess! Let's do this!" He pulled me into a hug and left his arm draped around my shoulders.

"I think I'm too nervous about it all to feel excited," I admitted to him—and myself.

"What are you nervous about?" he asked, as Charlie returned stick in mouth, tail wagging.

"What if I fail?" I answered with a sigh.

"If you fail," he said, looking at me directly, "at least you know you gave it your best shot, and you take some time to heal. And then you try again."

I knew we were both talking about multiple things, but he was right.

I had to know I tried.

It was for me, for the little girl with cancer who got to paint pictures and play games with people, and for the patients who would sob the morning away and then manage to laugh during jazz-ercise. It wasn't all just about the body dying, their organs shutting down, it was equal parts physical and mental.

He squeezed my shoulders again, bringing me back to the picnic table on the shoreline.

"If you fail," he said, and tilted my chin towards his own before kissing me softly, "I will help you get up again."

As we walked back to the loft, a few stars dotted the night sky. We both stopped in our tracks, the only one confused was Charlie, who looked around to see if the humans could sense something he had missed. He sat on the pavement and stared at the sky with us.

"Do you think she's there?" I heard him whisper.

"Yes, I think she's there." I pointed to the stars, then brought my finger to his chest and traced a circle over his heart. "And here too."

A lot of people didn't make it to the end of my story, that was just how life was, but I would always remember what page their names were on.

I would listen and learn from them all. They told me that going, living, was the most important thing at the end of the day.

And so I would go, with all of my heart.

CHAPTER THIRTY-TWO

Caspar

I had pictured this day from the moment we had started to plan it all. I had pictured being in the garden outside the hospital I had been a frequent flyer of the emergency room at. I had pictured my strange friend, with her bright pink glasses, in the front row sticking her tongue out at me to try and make me laugh. I pictured playing the songs that Ansa had inspired and telling her afterwards to let her know how much she meant to me.

I had pictured this moment, this entire day, being different than it ended up being.

It rained all day, it rained so much that I thought the tent may give way to the droplets at some point, and I worried about the piano which randomly showed up here this morning. The delivery guy had specific directions from the purchaser to deliver it to this address, and on this date, at this time.

Tessa didn't know who sent it and stood there baffled as she signed for the delivery. I had a feeling it had something to do with an old friend though, and when I opened the lid to check the tuning on the piano, there was a tiny note inside from the company it had been purchased from, with only one word scribbled on it.

Boo.

I told Tessa right away, and we both cried. Not quite tears of sadness, and not quite tears of joy, but somewhere in between.

The place itself was not the grandest in looks, but it looked like a place you could call home. It was quaint, it had a picket fence and was made of red bricks.

We busied ourselves with setting up chairs,

which had all been rented, while the tent was set up by the professionals at the rental company for us. We were ready with still a few hours to go before people started showing up, so when Lorraine arrived, Tessa took us on a tour.

The inside of the building was something out of a movie, somewhere a family of twenty could have lived comfortably. It looked lived in; it would definitely need a new coat of paint in the hallways, which Tessa volunteered both Lorraine and I to help with.

Lorraine and I looked at each other knowing-ly, laughing.

"What is so funny?" Tess turned around, hands on her hips.

"Just how you are already bossing us both around, and we haven't even started to work here yet!" Lorraine feigned horror at the idea of an even worse boss than the suits she had prior.

I interrupted the joke, confused. "Actually,

just one of us is working here…" Lorraine looked at Tessa, as confused as I was.

"You haven't asked him yet?" she questioned Tessa, who was wearing Herb's sweater with the green leprechaun on it. She said it was the only option for today.

"Tell me what?" I asked.

"Well, we are going to need more help around here. I didn't have time to ask you what with the whole moving in together, falling in love, losing friends, oh, plus a whole concert to put on—it's been a little busy. But Lorraine had a brilliant idea about you joining us here!"

I looked between them, bewildered. "Doing what?"

"Playing the piano, moving beds around, helping with maintenance around the building… That sort of stuff."

I heard Ansa in my head, telling me that life is too fast to not actually live it.

I thought about my nine to five, and I thought about the idea of going back there after all that had happened. I would owe my boss some good reasoning though, as he had been so generous with time off lately and had truly been understanding.

But I couldn't imagine saying no.

"Let's do it," I said, and in my pocket, wrapped my hand around the piece of paper with *Boo* scribbled on it.

The women looked at each other in surprise and then Tessa was squealing and had her arms wrapped around my body in a bear hug.

"I may have to take some courses on building maintenance though, I tried to fix my bike once and ended up needing a new bike."

Lorraine snorted at this and clapped a hand on my back.

We spent time talking about the future of the building, planning where certain things would be placed and what the days would look like. We would be working around the clock the next few months, in order to get to where we needed to be to open our doors to patients.

Suddenly, people were streaming into their seats outside.

Lorraine was the first to join the crowd, bidding us farewell for now but promising we would all be sick of each other within a few weeks. So that was something to look forward to.

Tessa was next, I pulled her in for a kiss and she wished me luck but told me I didn't need it. I had almost forgotten that this crowd was filled with people I had not played in front of in a long while; these were music people, these were people from what felt like a different lifetime.

I wondered if I would ever play piano in a professional capacity again, or if this was the last time I would ever be playing for this type of an audience.

I think I preferred the audience I had played

our dress rehearsal for, that was the real show after all. That was the show Ansa had heard, when I had so desperately willed the music to break through whatever was stopping her from being present with us. I played with such a desperation that night because I had played for her. I think that show was my goodbye. When she woke up and told me she had heard everything, it was as though I had already said everything I needed to say to her. Everything I needed to make sure she knew before she breathed her last breath.

I had another person who I had to say a proper farewell to though, someone who I knew would have given anything to hear me play one more song.

I changed into the traditional regalia I would wear when we participated in Indigenous events back home in Canada, an outfit of bright colours and feathers, one that had sat at the back of my closet ever since I had moved here and given up on everything.

I spent some time in the bathroom of our next adventure, the Rainbow Bridge.

I stared at myself in the mirror and braided my hair in the way my mother would have, and in the same way her mother would have done for her. I hoped someday I would braid my child's hair as well and tell them about their grandmother. I felt her presence when I looked in the mirror and had to grip the side of the sink to keep from falling. It was like a piece of me was missing all along, and I had just clicked it back into the spot that had been vacant for years.

I had never played the piano dressed like this because it wasn't typical in the realm of classical music.

Life was not meant to be typical, though. I thought of the pink glasses at the last minute and grabbed them from my backpack before hurrying outside.

It was crowded underneath the tent; we had

meant to have some people sit outside but the weather had ruined that idea, so there were guests standing in between the aisles. A hush fell over the crowd as people saw me emerge from the building.

I forgot that my name had been quite well-known in the industry. When I abruptly ended my career in music under the unfortunate circumstances, I never really thought that anyone would notice.

It was clear to me now that there were people who noticed. There were people who had paid money to come and see me, to hear me play, and I straightened my back to walk with pride.

Murmurs erupted no doubt in relation to my attire. I saw Tessa at the corner of the crowd, perched on a stool, making sure everything was going to plan with a bird's eye view of everything, and the smile on her face was contagious as it spread to my face instantly.

I took my seat at the piano bench and placed the pink glasses I held in my hand next to me, on the side of the bench that the crowd could not see.

I cleared my throat, and the crowd silenced immediately.

I had completely changed the song selection a few nights ago, after Ansa passed away. There was a night Tessa slept in my bed, and I realized I was truly happy for the first time since my mother left this earth, and I wanted to be able to tell her that I was okay.

The only person left for me to say goodbye to, the only thing I had left standing between me and my future, was grieving the loss of my mother.

So I played the songs we shared. I played renditions and pieces and bits of things from over the years, I played anything that reminded me of her.

Halfway through the set, there was a lull where I allowed my fingers to slow and built some intensity through the dramatic undertones in the notes. I had a chance to look up and saw there was so much happening in the crowd.

First, there were the fans who had tears running down their faces from the music itself.

Then, there was Tessa who stared at me in a way I wasn't sure I would ever be worthy of, but I was certain I would always strive to be. It was pure love, and I smiled at her. She knew the smile was for her, and I had to bite back laughter when I watched the way her cheeks went flush, I made mental note to tease her about it later—

There in the middle of the audience.

There were two women.

I felt muscle memory take over as I stared at the two women who were holding hands in the audience.

Ansa's hair was blonde, she looked so alive and healthy it was jarring to see her in the way she must have looked before I had known her. She had a pair of lime green glasses on. I watched in amazement as she winked at me and stuck her tongue out, exactly in the way I had imagined. I looked beside me to the pink glasses on the piano bench, and then quickly looked back to see who the other person was, and when the woman looked up, I felt my heart stop in my chest.

Mum?

My mother sat next to Ansa, hand in hand. Beaming.

Her hair was braided the same way mine was; she was an image of grace as she adorned the same traditional attire I wore and held her free hand to her heart.

I wanted to scream out to her, but instead I smiled at them and simply continued to play, willing myself to stay calm and live in this moment, accept this image for what it was. When the image blurred, and I could no longer make out their features, they went back to being two women who were wearing formal dresses and had grey hair and watched my piano more than me.

I closed my eyes and bowed my head, serene as I captured the image in my mind, confident I would be going back to it.

The final piece I played was a memorial to them both. The first half was notes from the song Ansa and I had played together at the piano in the lobby, and the second half combined notes from one of my mother's favourites, one that she had grown up hearing her father play.

As I played the song, I saw every note drifting up to the beyond, joining the stars that were there waiting for the sun to disappear so they could shine brightly.

I hunched over the keys and willed every feeling I had never let come to the surface after my mother's death to be left on the keys.

I remembered Tessa tracing a circle around my heart with her soft hands, and I knew she was right. They were both there, they were both with me even though I didn't know it sometimes, it just took me a while to realize it.

I wouldn't numb these feelings anymore, because numbing them meant numbing everything else too.

I knew my mother would have adored Tessa, in the same way Ansa had known we were right for one another.

As the final note faded, the crowd fell silent. Even the sniffles were hushed. I sighed and lifted my fingers off the keys and laid them on my lap.

I took a moment to enjoy the silence, to physically feel the weight be lifted from my shoulders, as I told my mother I was okay.

I was okay.

I would be okay.

It was okay for her to go; I would be okay.

The things I never got to say to her, the things I had always wondered if she knew. I willed them into my mind and sent them to the beyond along with the melodies that echoed out of the tent.

The moment of silence ended, and I straightened my back feeling the weight missing.

I stood, and bowed ever so slightly from my waist, and then the crowd erupted into cheers.

I couldn't hear anything though, because all I could see was Tessa standing in the front row, and right beside her—the two women, Ansa and my mother, clapping vigorously and bellowing cheers into my ears.

I could hear them, in my heart and in my soul.

I knew they wouldn't last long though, so I made sure to smile as I felt tears roll down my face, and I watched them hold hands once more, and walk out of the tent, somehow passing through the crowd with ease.

Boo, I could feel the note in my pocket and wondered if Ansa had orchestrated this moment as well, or if it was just my brain playing tricks on me.

Or maybe it was meant to be left unanswered.

I watched them go. Ansa disappearing into nothingness as my mother turned around and blew a kiss to me, before joining her.

Then Tessa was right beside me, hand in mine, and speaking into a microphone.

"We really want to thank everyone for their contributions, without you and your generous donations this would not have been possible. You are sitting outside of Whitegates' newest Hospice Care Home, The Rainbow Bridge. We will be fully operational in just a matter of a few months, something that once again, would not have been made possible if not for your generosity and compassionate giving. On behalf of all of us here at The Rainbow Bridge, thank you..."

I couldn't hear the rest; I was too focused on staring at the space in which I had seen my mother blow me a kiss. The space in which I had seen Ansa hold her hand. I found myself worried they would be gossiping about me in the beyond all the time. What a fun pairing that would be.

The event was over before I knew it, and Tessa and I were back home sitting on the porch.

Charlie sat between us as he always did now.

I scratched behind his ear and Tess rested her head on my shoulder.

The stars were out, and I couldn't help but think of the pink glasses that had started this whole adventure. I wondered if she had known where we would all end up. I wondered what she would think seeing us here now, and then I wondered if she somehow already knew.

I leaned over to kiss Tess on the head, her familiar presence comforting. Being with her felt like coming home after a long day at work. I found myself thinking about our future often, because I was excited for all the opportunities and adventures that lay ahead.

I sighed contentedly and smiled down at Tessa who was softly snoring. After the busy day we had I couldn't blame her, and I planned to carry her up the stairs and tuck her into the bed. But I wanted a few more moments of looking at the specks of starlight that illuminated the night sky.

I struck up a conversation with her in my head, as I had found myself doing recently on occasion because it made me feel close to her.

You always said you loved the stars, Ansa, and I grew to love them too.

It's funny how they seem to shine just a little bit brighter now that you've gone to join them.

ACKNOWLEDGEMENTS

I would like to acknowledge that the soil on which I wrote this piece of fiction is not my own. I would like to acknowledge the land on which I reside, and which the Region of Peel operates, is part of the Treaty Lands and Territory of the Mississauga's of the Credit. For thousands of years, Indigenous peoples inhabited and care for this land, and continue to do so today. In particular I acknowledge the territory of the Anishinabek, Huron-Wendat, Haudenosaunee, and Ojibway/Chippewa peoples; the land this is home to the Metis; and most recently, the territory of the Mississauga's of the Credit First Nation who are direct descendants of the Mississauga's of the Credit.

I am grateful to have the opportunity to work

on this land, and by doing so, give respect to its first inhabitants.

If you had told me a year ago we would be in a global pandemic and I would be helping families to say goodbye to their loved ones over Facetime calls, I would have laughed at the absurdity of the thought. If you had told me a year ago I would be put through one of the most mentally and physically draining eras to be working in the healthcare industry, well, I actually don't know if I would have done anything differently. Despite the fear, anxiety, depression, and endless swabs up the nostril, I would do it all again just because of the people I get to know.

If you had told me a month ago, when I embarked on this manuscript, that I would eventually be here, in the acknowledgements of a completed novel, I would have called you a liar as well and pointed you in the direction of the fifteen unfinished ones that sit in Microsoft Word and laugh at me when I start a new one.

The first person I have to thank here, is my-self. There have been many semi-colons along the way, but you keep fighting and I am proud of you.

Next, the person who managed to keep me from falling into an abyss of my own thoughts throughout the pandemic, my number one fan and cheerleader: Christopher, thank you for helping me to love myself more than I ever imagined I could, for showing me it's okay to take a break, but not to give up. You will always be my infinity.

Furthermore, the pink glasses of my life. The people who were shooting stars in my life, gone in the blink of an eye. Know that you live on in my memory and in my heart. I have been so honoured to get to listen to your stories and to get to be a small part of your life. I would like to share some of these lessons, these stories, and moments in time that I was lucky enough to hear first-hand with all of you who are reading this. If you'd like to read about some of the infinitely small things, the moments in time from my career as a Recreation Therapist and Social Services Worker, please continue to read the next section. And to the shooting stars of my life, thank you for teaching me all these things—I know you didn't know who I was on Earth, due to your diagnoses, but I like to think you all know me after you have passed on. I hope I will one day see you again. I hope you are at peace.

And finally, thank you for reading. For taking the time out of your day to read something that means a lot to this amateur author.

Always make time to take a wee dander in the park and jump in the puddles along the way.

INFINITELY SMALL THINGS

I have worked in the field of geriatric social work for what feels like a thousand years after the whole COVID-19 pandemic but what is in actuality closer to five years. It may sound like the blink of an eye, but the relationships and people I got to foster and care for on a daily basis will always be a part of who I am. Most of my career has been focused on caring for people with diagnosed dementias, but that word does not define them. Instead, the following are small lessons I have learned from my real-life Ansa's…

Live as though it is your last day, every day.

This lesson is a constant, one that I cannot pinpoint to any one particular person, but it is something shared amongst most people who are at the end of their lives. This is not to say, live with reckless abandon. Don't go jumping off cliffs (unless you know how to do that kind of stuff, and want to, I guess?). If you love someone though, tell them. If you disagree with something, say it respectfully. Fight for what you believe in. Never go to bed angry. Book that vacation and buy a cake for yourself just because. At the end of your life, the small things end up making up something much bigger in your head and heart. Make sure you take time to work on yourself, and to reflect. Life is not meant to be watched, it is meant to be lived, whatever that means for you in your own dreams.

Never stop learning.

I met a woman once who was 91 and learned how to play the guitar. You are never too old to pick up something new, never too busy to fit five minutes of learning into your schedule. Download an app to teach you Spanish or sign yourself up for Latin Dance classes. You never know what talents and hidden gems are getting hidden by the monotony of our modern world. We always feel like breaking from the routine; what we know is too scary and anxiety inducing. So lean into that anxiety and let it drive you.

I am woman, hear me roar.

To the woman who taught me what feminism is, and what it means to be a woman. R, you would sing and dance like nobody was watching. "Shake it baby, shake it!"

Create.

J, the man who we didn't understand at first. You seemed upset all the time until we discovered your past and who you were. You seemed unapproachable until I set you up with a dollar store paint set, and you managed to make me something that belongs in the Louvre. It's on my bookshelf, and I bring it to staff education seminars. I tell them to make sure they understand the person behind the behaviour, always. I tell them about you.

Be proud of who you are, and where you

come from.

To I, the one who taught me all about my heritage and slang across Ireland. "Yer heads a Marley, and yer cracked like an egg, but I love you." I know you always wanted out of that blasted joint, and I hope you one day laugh at how I would try and distract you from how frustrating things were for you. Your spirit burned bright, and I hope one day to be just as incredible of a person as you.

There are so many more lessons. There are some that are too close to my heart to share or to mean anything to anyone who didn't live them. I think that's the ultimate perspective here though; live your life with utmost appreciation for the fact that it is fleeting. Make every moment count and take time to enjoy the little things.

To all my teachers, the ones who are still here with me, the ones whose hands I held as they passed on, and the ones who I have yet to meet—thank you. Thank you, from the bottom of my heart, for making

me into the person I am today and helping me recognize that the beauty in death itself is how it pushes us
to live with more passion.

397

Thank you, thank you, thank you.